BILLBOARD MAN

BILLBOARD MAN

JIM FUSILLI

The characters and events portrayed in this book are fictitious. Any similarity to real persons, living or dead, is coincidental and not intended by the author.

Printed in the United States of America.

Published by Thomas & Mercer

PO Box 400818

Las Vegas, NV 89140

ISBN-13: 9781612181936

ISBN-10: 1612181937

Library of Congress Control Number: 2013901097

To Ralph, Jessica, Franny

and Ally Pezzullo

1

He was driving north across Arizona, the sun baking the rental car as it roared past Joshua trees and prickly pears. Purple veins in the mesas rose and dipped, disappeared and returned. Buttes surged toward wispy clouds. As he rolled down a window, the scent of sage and rosemary surrounded him, stirring thoughts of his childhood. The wind ruffled his sandy hair.

He stopped on the roadside and cut the engine. The air conditioner sputtered and died. In an instant, his skin felt like parchment paper. He stepped outside; hands on hips, he stretched his back, cracked his knees. He looked around to find a jackrabbit or a bark scorpion. There were familiar faces in the rock formations.

Returning to his seat, he examined himself in the rearview mirror, ran his tongue along his new porcelain bridge. He'd taken a beating a little while ago and he wondered if he was still recovering. He had a new scar on his lip. The old one alongside his eye looked like a teardrop. He was 41 years old and though he kept a phone within arm's reach, there was little chance anyone would call. His wife was dead, and no one said it was his fault but the person who mattered most. He drove off, clicking the seat belt as he bumped onto blacktop.

Phoenix had suited him. It was busy with its own plans. People moved with purpose. They were caught up in their own ideas. The place wasn't made yet. It wasn't finished. Construction crews worked through the night, and he watched as they put another floor on an office tower. Cranes swung overhead. Pile drivers shook the grit beneath his feet. He watched pearl pebbles quiver and quake. Nobody cared if he was there. A lizard scooted across his foot.

When he couldn't sleep the day away, the unrelenting sun squeezing past water-stained window shades, he'd ride the light-rail system. It had 28 stops. He'd settle in and watch the city roll by. Now and then, he dozed off. At certain depots, crowds poured in and he gave up his seat, bracing himself against the ceiling with his long fingers. The air-conditioning rushed past his shirt collar. "Thank you kindly," one woman said, a bitty thing, bow-legged, sloe-eyed and solemn. He nodded. Later he realized she was the only person to speak to him in two days.

At the airport depot, everybody struggled with luggage. He helped when it was needed. Kids were skittish with excitement and trepidation. They had no idea what could happen. They looked at their fathers with unalloyed trust. It was a long step down to the sidewalk. They held out their little hands. It broke his heart.

One afternoon it was so hot the buttons on his shirt stung his skin.

He stumbled across a storefront restaurant on Van Buren, not too far from the furnished apartment he took on a 30-day lease. When he was 14 years old, he worked in a place just like it up in Philo. Both restaurants had good green-chili sauce and generous portions. Here in Phoenix, he drank a Negra Modelo or two, pushed salty chips through salsa, ordered flautas, his elbows on a plastic tablecloth. He did the same thing two or three times, reading a paperback through the meal. The busboy said, "Hey, bro. That's a new book, no?" He decided it was time to go. He left five oxford shirts at a Chinese laundry, a blazer and his other pair of jeans in a closet.

Most times, he walked into a train station, looked at the board and bought a ticket—summer up north, winter down south. This time he decided to rent a car. He wanted to see the Grand Canyon again and gaze at piñon pines. He'd climb over a guardrail and, treading carefully, cradle in a hidden crevice, allowing himself to fall out of time. At night, he would reach out and hold the stars in the palm of his hand.

Then he'd double back and sleep the daylight away in Flagstaff, where he'd buy new shirts and a blazer, a couple pairs of jeans. He'd been in Flagstaff before, driving toward New Mexico, once again fleeing California, this time for an entirely different and once unimaginable reason: "Dad, go," Pup said, holding back tears. "Just go." That was three years ago, more or less. Back then, he didn't know how to disappear. He didn't know how to live only in a moment or beat back his loneliness. He'd walked Arizona for hours, the heat relentless until the sun was gone. He arrived at Sunset Crater after midnight and knelt to run his hand across the basalt on the lava flow trail. A park ranger nudged him awake; he'd fallen asleep at the base of a volcano.

Now he left Flagstaff and drove south as if he were returning to Phoenix. But then he turned off the highway, climbed high and pulled into an old copper-mining camp that came back as a hub for artists and antique dealers. It had a dusty two-story flatiron building, and when he turned a corner through the twilight he could see forever, adobe and sky blue. Down the end of the block was a bar with a few motorcycles out front. He needed a shower and a shave, but he figured the crowd, such as it was, wouldn't mind if he had a burger and a beer. He nestled in the corner at the end of the bar by the front window, away from the taps, and soon the burly bartender took his order. A couple of guys were shooting pool under a lazy ceiling fan. From around the corner, musicians were loading equipment onto the little platform stage in back, and he could imagine the room filling up tonight and everybody having a fine time, everybody acquainted with everybody else. He decided he'd eat quickly and go.

He looked at his phone, a prepaid. He opened his book. The beer arrived in an icy mug. A while later, the burger turned up and he ordered another beer. A few more people came in. They looked at him and moved on.

"Hey," she said.

She was tall and hearty, and her honey-brown hair framed her face. She was maybe just short of 30, and all that time in the sun hadn't done her skin a bit of harm. She wore a white, long-sleeved T rolled to the elbows, snug jeans and soft, musty boots.

He wiped his mouth with a paper napkin. "Hey."

"Good book?"

He slid it across the bar toward her and of course she sat, one leg up, the other long and inviting.

"Might be too much for me," she said after flipping a few pages.

He sipped his beer.

The bartender brought a longneck to her.

"Ginger," she said.

"J.J.," he told her. It was the name he used in Phoenix.

"Where are you from, J.J.? No. Let me guess."

The driver's license in his wallet said he lived in Toronto, Indiana. He'd never been there.

She turned on the bar stool and closed one sienna eye. "California," she said finally.

"Big state."

"Northern California."

"How come?"

"The hair," she said, gesturing. "The way it just sort of falls. And you don't burn, do you? The wind takes care of you."

He shrugged.

She had a cocky little smile. "Don't ask me where I'm from."

He denied himself just about everything he once loved. But it turned out there was something about a certain kind of woman he could not resist. He was thinking she might be one of them.

"Settle in," he suggested.

"I already have."

Nighttime and the place was filling up, but the band hadn't started yet. Some kind of old Southern rock played from the jukebox, and they were still talking about nothing. Ginger dropped her hand on top of his. "The next round's mine," she said.

He stood and nodded toward the back of the bar.

"I'll save your place," she said as she started thumbing through his book again.

A wiry guy sitting by the pool table watched him as he made the long walk to the restroom.

When he came out, the guy was in his seat at the bar. He was barking at Ginger.

"You're in my seat," said the man who'd introduced himself to the woman as J.J.

"Nobody's talking to you, Dad."

Dad?

The wiry guy had sideburns along his narrow face and a little thatch of hair under his bottom lip. He wore black jeans and thick boots with heels for stomping. His studded leather wristband matched his belt, and colorful tattoos marred his arms like half-done graffiti.

"Boone—"

"Let's get going, Ginger," he demanded as he slid down off the stool. "Enough's enough."

"Boone," she repeated. "Do you mind?"

He grabbed her arm. "Come on."

Ginger snapped free.

J.J. stepped between them. "She'll see you later, Boone."

"Old man, you don't know what you're trying to bite off."

J.J. edged toward the stool. Trying to turn down the heat, he said, "Your friend just bought me a beer."

Boone Stillwell was on his way to drunk but hadn't gotten there yet. "Who said she's my friend?"

"She's got the right to see me put it away."

"You think this is funny, old man?"

Not yet, no.

"Do you?"

"Boone," Ginger said. "Why are you doing this? Boone."

Boone made some kind of move and out of his back pocket came a leather band, rounded on top and weighted.

"Oh shit. No, Boone," Ginger moaned.

J.J. Walk took a beating not long ago with a lead sap. Thing bit like a son of a bitch. A double shot could crack bone.

Interested now, the crowd inched forward. The clack of pool balls halted.

Boone raised the sap up high and rolled his wrist like he was preparing to strike.

"Is it funny now, old—"

The beer mug smashed Boone Stillwell full force in the face and slammed him back into the door frame. J.J. dove off the stool, the mug still in his hand, and, kneeling on Stillwell, hit him with it square on the forehead, using the mug like brass knuckles. Second time he hit him, the mug shattered. J.J. looked down and he had the handle in his fist.

A shard of glass was embedded in Stillwell's face, just above the eyebrow.

J.J. jumped up.

He looked at the sap, which also served as a key chain, three or four keys on the ring.

He kicked it toward a corner.

He spun, waiting, legs wide, fists cocked. A crowd had gathered near, maybe 15 people including the bikers from down the bar.

First time he was pounded to paste in public, he was 15 years old.

Now a big leather-vest biker with a handlebar mustache pointed to his neck. "Say, friend…"

The man who called himself J.J. dropped the handle and felt for a piece of glass stuck near his own throat.

He pulled it clear.

"Ginger," the bartender said, "get him out of here."

Her T-shirt was soaked with beer.

Stillwell was bleeding from his mouth where the first blow struck. A thin stream oozed from the wound above his brow. His eyes rolled in his head.

Composed, Ginger said, "J.J., let's go."

He was surprised. He thought the bartender was telling her to get Stillwell out of his doorway.

"J.J." She was tugging at his sleeve.

He had $43 in his pocket. He tossed the bills on the bar.

He grabbed his book and followed Ginger through the crowd toward the side door.

"We'll take my car," she said as they trotted into the arid night air.

He shook his head. He was done here.

"J.J."

He had a gun in the glove compartment, a Glock 17. But no one in the bar had followed them outside.

"I'm just saying we'd better go," Ginger said, tugging at his arm. "He'll be all right. But still..."

He looked over his shoulder.

She smiled and gestured to her beer-soaked T. "You don't want to remember me like this, do you?" There was a note of hope in her voice.

He could feel blood trickling down his neck.

He walked toward his rental. She followed, then waited by the shotgun door.

The twisting highway had him going back the way he came and then it headed east again, and she said, "Where do you live?"

He hadn't had a fixed address in years. Back then, he'd rented an apartment near UCLA, about a half mile from where his daughter stayed. Her agent sent him a message that told him she'd gotten a temporary restraining order that said he had to stay 500 feet away.

"I'm on the road," he said.

She went "Mmmm."

She mentioned a town up ahead about 5 miles.

They drove in silence for a bit, the road demanding his attention. Red-rock spires pierced the star-speckled sky.

When they came around a curve to a long straightaway, there wasn't another car in front or coming up behind.

Inside the rental, the dashboard lights gave off a little green glow.

"You have any music, J.J.?" Ginger said. Before he could reply, she popped the glove compartment.

The Glock sat on a copy of *The Hollywood Reporter.*

She withdrew his gun. She hefted it in her hand.

"Well..."

The clip was under his seat, but there was a round in the chamber.

"Are you a cop?"

He shook his head.

Before returning the gun to its station, she looked at the magazine. A story was circled. A film in preproduction.

"In the movie business?" she asked.

"What do you say we keep it simple," he replied. "All right by you?"

She reached over and ran her thumb along his outer ear.

"Sure. Simple."

Afterward, the sheets twisted and kicked to the floor, she purred as she slept. Toward dawn, she let out a little laugh but didn't wake. He sat by the hotel room window and watched the sun rise bright and ready to bake the desert sand. In the distance, snow capped the sprawling mountains.

He was thinking there was something off about that kid he'd knocked out. Boone Stillwell was nobody's idea of a tough guy. The sap was a joke, a toy. It could've ended without blood. He could've said, OK, you win. I'm gone.

Would've made the kid's year.

"Don't think for a minute you're putting me in a taxi," she said when she came out of the shower. It was midmorning. He'd made the bed, wriggled under the covers and dozed off.

He elbowed up and said, "I'm going east."

"All right. But you're going west first."

Then she jumped into bed and he felt her warm skin as she kissed his lips, kissed his neck and reached under the top sheet.

During the night, he turned on her phone and saw she'd gotten nine calls, all from the same source. That kid Boone, no doubt. He shuffled the number to his memory.

Now they drove without purpose. She found a radio station. A plucked guitar and whistling accordion followed them into a town. They had lunch at a sun-soaked rooftop cantina, sharing sopaipillas and icy beer. The waitress stared at the bloodstains on his collar and shirtfront.

"What's on your mind?" Ginger asked.

He said he couldn't stand the clothes he was wearing. It was to her credit that she'd rinsed her soggy top in warm water and hung it on the hotel balcony's rail. Sitting in the sun, it'd dried fast and smelled like a new day.

She pointed down a street crowded with shops.

"Maybe," he said. He didn't care to tell her he bought his shirts in one particular store, his jeans in another, T-shirts in yet another. There was a brand of shaving cream he preferred.

She was a fine-looking woman. He saw that she figured how to get by in her own skin and stay sweet. She had a hell of a smile and he was going to have to work hard to forget that song she hummed while she washed his hair.

"So…You drift, huh?" she said.

"I drift."

"I'd ask why, but you wouldn't tell me."

No.

"You go a long way to read a book you could read at home," she said.

He nodded. "That's about it."

"And you carry a gun."

"I wouldn't make a thing out of it."

"You're an actor."

"I am not an actor."

She laughed. "I'm annoying you..."

He shook his head.

"Well, you won't have to put up with me too much longer if you don't want to. By the way, I'm on at midnight."

He drank the cold beer until the bottle was empty.

"You're supposed to ask, On what? Or where?"

"On what? Where?"

He dropped her off before sunset up the block from the bikers' bar in the old mining town and waited as she snuggled in behind the wheel of her silver compact. To grab a note left on her windshield, she flicked on the wipers and caught it on the first pass. He noticed she read it, then threw it down without a second thought.

She'd given him an address out on the highway. "But you won't come..." she'd said as she stole a kiss before stepping out.

He found a mall about halfway back to Phoenix. He couldn't get the oxford shirts he liked, but he picked up four T-shirts and a navy crew-neck sweater to ward off the autumn chill. Found the jeans he wanted too and bought two pairs. They fit just right, snug and down on his hips.

He had a little kit bag in the trunk. He retrieved it and washed in the restroom, scrubbing his face and under his arms, and dried with paper towels. He peeled the Band-Aid off the cut on his neck. Thing was healing fine.

2

Francis Cherry sat behind his desk in his oak-lined office. Bored witless, he flipped a 1933 U.S. Gold Double Eagle: heads, tails, tails, heads. He paid $8.5 million for it. Used to belong to King Farouk. The tie he wore at half-mast cost $6, bought from a street vendor. He'd had an emu egg for breakfast, served in his private dining room that overlooked the corner of Wall and Broad Streets. He peppered it from a little packet he picked up at the U.S. Open near the old World's Fair grounds in Queens.

Only the third week in October and already he'd earned more than he did last year. He'd had an even dozen weeks in which he'd scored $50 million in fees. Yep.

Seeking his advice, the seven-member President's Economic Council of Botswana waited in one conference room, a former officer of the International Monetary Fund in another, the young, soon-to-be-divorced wife of the president of Euronext NV and her lawyers in a third. They were among the very many who had yet to fathom that Cherry's private financial counsel could be boiled down to two sentences: "Wait for the tell" was one. The other: "There's always an errant hair in the soup."

Cherry ran his hand over his shaved head and buzzed his secretary, the former president of an employment agency specializing in superior office-management talent. Cherry paid Mrs. Brent $15,000 a week with a bonus of $100,000 due at year's end.

Now 76 years old and close to deaf, as a young woman Elsa Brent had been a secretary to Junius Spencer Morgan III, grandson of J.P. Morgan. Cherry figured she was a guarantee against trouble he didn't need. Secretaries had a way of soiling his day. Apparently, he could be difficult.

"Mrs. Brent," he said as she entered lean and stately, steno book in hand. Morgan gave her that Conway Stewart fountain pen.

She stared at his lips.

"Get me the words to the national anthem of Botswana; the FBI file on what's his name, the IMF guy; and book a private room at Masa and tell them it'll be two for dinner at nine. Then tell Mrs. Euronext she's coming—alone."

"Yes, Mr. Cherry," she said, her voice a high, nasal whine. She turned to leave.

To her back, Cherry said, "Find out if Morton Downey Jr. is still alive and tell him I'll give him six hundred thousand dollars if he'll tattoo my name on his forehead."

When Mrs. Brent failed to respond, Cherry stomped his foot so she'd feel the vibration. He liked the old coot. She had style. She was the rare person he worked with who didn't fear him.

"Yes?" Turning, she placed a hand on a leather club chair for balance.

"If you wouldn't mind," said Francis Cherry, "please tell Goldsworthy I'll be leaving in ten minutes."

At a food court upstairs at the South Street Seaport, Ian Goldsworthy paced as he waited for his boss to arrive, thoughts colliding or dribbling to an end before completion. On a table for six that had a postcard view of the Brooklyn Bridge sat three large orders of Nathan's French fries and a '98 Château Valandraud Saint Emilion. Otherwise, the table was empty. When fanny-packed tourists approached, eager to put down their overloaded trays, Goldsworthy rose up in a way that sent them directly to the airport for the next flight home. At least I can still scare off a few Americans, he thought.

A former MI6 operative in his early 50s, silver-haired Goldsworthy looked much older, thanks to a life of considerable misadventure and self-abuse. He was Cherry's head of security, charged with gathering intelligence on members of the financial and business communities. It was a job for which he was ill suited, he being of the school wherein clipping off nipples with pruning shears in a third-world jungle hut got a bloke what was needed.

Here, he had no advantage: Wall Street was rife with men and women who also were once part of the international security apparatus. When MI6 cut him loose and banished him to the States—dredging up as a pretext accusations of his taste for black-tar heroin and Malaysian houseboys—they told him if he landed a corporate security post, he' d be competing against retired cops, potbellied and wrung dry. Second week on Wall Street he saw, eating an orange Popsicle outside the Stock Exchange, an ex-Kuwaiti commando, a man who had tipped the U.S. First Brigade to Saddam Hussein's spider hole in ad-Dawr. Goldsworthy knew he' d been outmaneuvered by suits in Vauxhall Cross. The gentry at SIS headquarters had gotten themselves the last laugh.

"Did you find him?" Francis Cherry asked as he sat.

Ian Goldsworthy replied, "We've made progress, Mr. Cherry."

"In other words, nothing," Cherry said, his mouth already full. "Are you trying?"

"We are trying, yes."

Sun shining on his head, Cherry gulped the rich red wine. "I'm thinking you're not."

"If you would allow me to explain—"

"There are these guys," Cherry said, "and they think that the word *explain* means they can start in with the excuses."

"We are making progress. But—"

"Ah. Thus warned, you endeavor to explain. Tell me what you know."

His back to plump clouds high above the bridge's cathedral towers, Goldsworthy said, "Mr. Cherry—"

"Hold on." Steam rose as Cherry took a bite of a salty Nathan's fry, then chewed with his eyes shut, the taste permeating his being to his soul.

"Continue."

"Sir, I—"

"Stop. You know nothing. Why not say that? I know nothing. Or: Though I have the man's fingerprints, nothing. Even: Though I claim to have fostered revolution with every third Joe and Joanie in the global spy machine—NSA, KGB, Mossad, Mukhabarat—and I am billing you for outside services and consultants, I. Still. Know. Nothing."

"We're—"

"I mean, here's a man who walks the streets. He takes public transportation. That shirt he wore when we met? Brooks Brothers, and laundered, Chinese style. Are there an infinite number of Brooks Brothers outlets and Chinese laundries? No, there are not."

Cherry paused for another bite. He sighed in delight. Then he frowned.

"I assume he also drives a car," he said, frying oil glistening on his lips. "He has a phone, he uses the Internet. You know, modus operandi."

"He's got himself a system, certainly," Goldsworthy managed, "and I'm sure it can be deciphered."

"I'm thinking no, it can't," Cherry said. "As in, you won't find him."

They sat in silence, Cherry watching a tug churn the river water to white, an arrow trail in its wake. Not long ago, he'd instructed Goldsworthy to recover items a former secretary had stolen from his private office safe. Goldsworthy farmed out the assignment and disaster ensued: bodies; police in three states; attempted blackmail; and the emergence of a man who called himself John Bleak, an avenging angel sort who cleaned up a botched job, then disappeared. This Bleak was a regular Mr. Can Do. As opposed to Ian Goldsworthy. Cherry once thought a man disreputable enough to have been booted from British secret intelligence would harbor the traits required for the occasional unsavory assignment. Alas, not so.

Cherry finished the final fry and licked his fingertips.

Seconds ticked. Goldsworthy, who'd once stared down the barrel of a G3 in Mombasa, couldn't bring himself to glance at his boss.

Cherry stood. His paper napkin fluttered to the sticky floor.

"Let's be clear," he said. "You've had weeks. Months. So this is the shot: Find the guy now."

"Sir, I'm not sure—"

Cherry started toward the escalator. Crystal decanter in hand, Goldsworthy hurried to follow.

"I can't make it any clearer," Cherry said as he wiped the corners of his mouth with a thumb and forefinger. "John Bleak. In my office. Yesterday."

"Why?"

"'Why'?"

They stepped onto descending stairs. "I don't mean to question you. But yes," said Goldsworthy. "Why? How can it matter?"

"All right. What the hell." Cherry clapped his hands together. "This guy we're talking about? Killer of killers? He holds it against me. Your mistake. The whole thing. The girl, the beatings, the blood. The bodies. Your mistake. He holds it against me. Me. You think I need an enemy like that?"

"But there's no evidence he killed anyone."

"You can take that risk. Me? I'm not you."

The escalator whooshed them to ground level. Cherry's driver was waiting on South Street, a crowd ogling his new black Rolls-Royce Ghost.

"This guy is a guy I want on my side. Get it?"

Goldsworthy watched as Cherry's chauffeur brushed through the crowd and opened a rear door. Cherry slipped inside. Soon the Ghost headed south toward Wall Street. The crowd dispersed, including one African-American kid who looked like the 13-year-old who pointed a rifle at Goldsworthy in Mombasa. Goldsworthy had severed his jugular vein, stowed the body under the Makupa Causeway, then swore to the boy's mother Her Majesty's highest priority was to find the killer. Two days later, he arrived in Mahajanga on his way to Mauritius.

Now Goldsworthy stepped into the shadows under the FDR Drive overpass. He was at the tipping point. Cherry wanted to offer Bleak a job that would likely carve into Goldsworthy's turf. In short order, they'd be rivals, and perhaps Bleak or whatever his name might be was better equipped for the kind of white-collar work Cherry required.

Why find the man who could do you in?

Yet: If I don't find Bleak, I'm out of a bloody job.

If he was out of a job, Goldsworthy would be on his own. Without Cherry's protection, he'd have to fend for himself. Soon he'd be working as a night watchman or a limo driver on the midnight-to-dawn shift. Fuck me, thought Ian Goldsworthy.

As he took a long, slow joyless swallow of Bordeaux blend, he realized, as it often was with Francis Cherry, there was no way to win.

Boone Stillwell arrived a half hour early at the tired diner off 89A, its neon sputtering against the Arizona night sky. He drove across its lot, a stony niche surrounded by creosote bush and sagebrush, and parked deep in a dark corner by a Dumpster, certain the son of a bitch who coldcocked him with a beer mug was about to show. Ginger had a way of enticing them to stick around. When they did, she'd think the newcomer was about to jump all-in and produce a ticket for her to tag along when it was time to go. She believed in that kind of whirlwind romance shit when in point of fact, and everybody knows this, you were supposed to end up with who you were destined to be with since you were kids: your high school sweetie, who knew your family and all your peculiar ways.

And yet there's Ginger, hoping for a better life, some fairy tale with chiffon and stardust and begonias and violins and whatnot. To Stillwell, it didn't make a lick of sense. A better life? How? They had everything they needed in town, firstly jobs—they loved her here at the Restful, and the county water company where he worked paid good and steady plus health insurance. They had friends, some from kindergarten even, meaning roots. Plus, from his point of view, also there was a bar with a pool table, a decent jukebox and somebody to blow you a beer every payday eve. A full deck, in other words.

He checked the pistol, an old EIG six-shooter, and waited, the yellow moon so clear in the night sky he could read the craters on its surface.

Ginger arrived a few minutes before midnight, her old silver compact crunching shale and shards until it settled. By then, only five cars remained in the lot.

In her black-and-white waitress uniform and white rubber-soled shoes, a little black sweater over her shoulders, she walked not into the café but across the gravel toward his dark corner of the lot. Boone saw moonlight flicker in her honey-brown hair.

He had butterfly stitches on his eyebrow and his mouth was swollen.

"Get inside," she said.

"I'll wait."

"He's not coming."

"He might. And it ain't none of your business now. You chose your side."

She chuckled. "Listen to you, blubbing like that. You sound like a dentist shot you full of Novocain."

"Leave me alone."

"Boone, when are you going to grow up? That's what I' d like to know."

To dismiss her, he waggled the gun.

"Your daddy's pistol."

"He don't need it no more, does he?"

"Change your mind about taking him on with your keys?"

He said, "Ol' Buddy here will do nicely, thank you."

Everyone in town knew he held on to the pistol like a special keepsake, treating it like it was the old man's photo in a silver locket. Ol' Buddy had a white grip you could see in the dark.

Boone Stillwell had loved his old man and, as his father lay ashen and cancer-withered, he transferred that affection to his high school sweetie. Ginger, who was looking to settle down, was 21 when they were married, Boone a year younger. A debacle; no surprise, seeing as hopeful and hapless always were a poor mix. "You're gaining a daughter, Daddy," Stillwell said to the barely alive body. Truth, though, was Ginger gained herself a 20-year-old son. "I need someone to take care of *me* now and again," she told him when she packed to leave. "I need a man."

"I'm a man," replied Boone Stillwell, naked except for Spider-Man briefs and eating cereal out of the box, milk dripping onto the throw rug.

Now Ginger flicked a thumb toward the diner. "Get inside," she repeated. "I'll make you a cup of coffee. You think you can chew some pie?"

The Restful had about a dozen vinyl-topped stools at a long counter. Wooden booths lined the opposite wall at the windows and curled around back by the restrooms. Peak hour on a busy night, the place might attract 40 people. It had three customers now. Grizzled retirees, moth-bitten flannel and tuft-like beards, they all knew Boone Stillwell, as did the departing four-to-midnight waitress, a Yavapai-Apache named Cotillion. The consensus: Pity poor Ginger. Girl with her looks and spunk deserved better than that sorry ass.

Ginger told her ex to hold tight. A few seconds later, she swung through the kitchen door and returned with an apron slung around her waist, a little pad in its pocket, a pencil tucked behind her ear. She slid a coffee cup along the Formica counter, then filled it with steaming brew.

"Wait eight hours," she said. "Maybe he's a morning person."

"If he don't show," Stillwell said, "I'll find him. Old bastard."

"I hate to tell you, but there's nothing old about him."

"He'll be old when I'm through with him. If he ain't dead, that is."

Exasperated, Ginger said, "And just how are you going to find him, Boone? Don't you think if he was findable, I' d go after him?"

"His name is J.J. and he drives a Kia with Cali plates."

"Boone, I was in the car, remember?"

"I got the plate number."

"No you don't."

"Most of it," he said. "There was an *H* in there."

"Well, there you go," she said. "He's in your sights."

"That's the last time somebody coldcocks me in my town."

For expediency's sake, Ginger softened. "Boone, you have many attributes. A fighter, though, you are not."

"He won't catch me off guard this time," he replied. "I'm strategized."

"Good luck," Ginger said as she walked the coffeepot down the aisle, a courtesy to the graybeard regulars.

He was going to tell her that everybody in the bar was laughing at him when he rose, wobbly, blood dribbling, his ass freshly kicked by a man with a book, the love of his life running off. And the laughter wasn't the "ha-ha, didn't you put on a show, arm across the shoulder, let me buy you a beer to perk up your spirits" kind. It was more a dismissive cackle that announced the presence of a full-fledged stooge. "That ain't the way to win her back," said the bartender as he gave him a Harley rag full of ice.

He decided he'd regain his place of pride by coming back with the old man's scalp on his belt.

In the modern way, of course.

He'd whap him good with Ol' Buddy's pearl handle and then, after he whapped him a few more times, he'd take his damned book, soak it in blood, drive it back across the state line and drop it on the bar where he'd sat.

Yes, sir.

Admiration would follow. Ginger would hear about it. Mmmm, she'd go. Maybe my Boone has changed his ways.

"Ready for that pie yet, killer?" she said as she passed.

3

He liked Memphis, Tennessee. At night, he stood on the bluff and listened to the river rush and churn. Or he explored the arboretum, losing himself under a canopy of thick winding branches that banished the sky. For the hell of it, he walked to Memphis, Mississippi. He left the Glock in his room.

When he couldn't sleep away the day, he rode the trolleys, watching the city roll by. He decided he'd go to Sun Studio where Elvis and the others cut their hits. Ninety-two degrees and there wasn't another soul walking on Union Avenue. He arrived after the tour began and was stuck in back, memorabilia in glass cases all around. Taller than the rest, he caught the guide's eye. The years had coated her in a hard shell, and her hair was dyed midnight black. She nodded ever so slightly to let him know she saw him, yes she did. She had a chip in a front tooth, and he liked the way she hooked her thumbs on her belt loops, framing her wide hips. When it was time to turn the group around to move downstairs, he was suddenly first in line. "And so on and so forth," she whispered to him as she passed, and as he took in her scent he thought of the raw earth beneath an oak tree. As everyone was leaving the gift shop, she told him her name was Lola, and they agreed they'd meet up at a joint on Beale. She smiled a little wicked to herself as he walked off, knowing she was free to get what she wanted, at least for the night. Her boyfriend, Joe Blunt, was off on a drug run down near the Bayou Macon, oxy in ample supplies. He mightn't be back for days. She'd have time off from his ferocious disposition and the clack of those damned sticks.

He went back to his room, read for a while, then shaved and showered, put on a fresh white oxford and a new pair of jeans he picked up en route. Whenever he stepped inside down south, he noticed they let the air-conditioning run high, so he slipped into his blue blazer. In the outfit that was his uniform since he took to the road, he saw in the rusted mirror the man he'd become, new scars and all. He'd told her his name was J.J. "J.J.," he said to his reflection.

On the walk over, he found himself thinking about her. Lola had a throaty rasp in her voice, but when she said her name she let the two short syllables unwind like honey off a spoon. When they were through, he'd get up and go, and he knew that would suit her fine. She was counting on nothing. She'd say, So long, J.J. He'd say, So long, Lola. Walking away had become a kind of expertise, or so he thought.

The bar was up the block under a snaking neon sign. It was early: Beale Street hadn't yet turned into a carnival. A cop on the corner cradled a shotgun.

He stepped inside. Lola crooked a finger to call him over. She kissed him to stake her claim, let her hip linger against his thigh. The jukebox blared. They found a booth; she faced the door. She wore a purple blouse. Cold longnecks arrived. A shot? she asked. Why not? Here's to the King, she said as they lifted their glasses and threw back smooth smoky-wood bourbon. He asked questions; she replied; soon it was all parry and thrust. They knew where this was going. Tell me about yourself, J.J. Not much to tell. Oh, you're one of those you-are-where-you-are types. He nodded; he said I guess that's about it. Lola raised her hand and let out a little shout. Do us again, would you, Billie? And Billie returned with two more beers, two more shots. Relaxing, they laughed. She ran the back of her hand along his cheek. He stared at her lips, at that little chip in her tooth. Yeah, she said, you're just about all right. On the way to her car, they kissed and soon they bounced into her bed down by the river and he found that scar on the inside of her thigh and listened as she groaned, her heavy breasts slapping and swaying, her hands groping to clutch the sheets or latch on to the headboard.

Later, he traced the five-point star she had tattooed on her backside. How could he know Lola's man Joe Blunt considered it his brand.

He left the bed to study the stars, stepping over a frayed throw rug. He felt a bit off, ill at ease. He couldn't say why. He liked it fine; she had her ways and in the midst of it all, she was gone, her eyes rolled up in her head. He was thinking about that now, and the way she bit hard on her bottom lip. Down below her, his back arched, hips high, he was a thing. When she slid off, he was thinking it was more like a tussle than a tender exchange. Soon she went off to sleep.

He surveyed the two-room space, the kitchen and the living room bleeding into one. Her clothes were scattered here and there, and a crocheted blanket was in a ball on the floor. A chest of drawers she might've picked up at a yard sale wore a candle that had burned down to a mass of wax nothing. He thought he detected the scent of marijuana lingering in the room.

A man lived here too, at least part of the time. She' d done her best to hide him, but more than a trace lingered. He wondered if the man had a key. Probably so.

Back in his shorts and shirt, he stood in the same spot until he forgot where he was.

She called him again, and then a third time, before he turned around.

She pulled back her damp dark hair and she said, "Hell of a time for a walk..."

He turned and saw her looking him over, fingers locked behind her head, the top sheet down by her waist.

"So, you old hound dog, what's your real name?"

Hound dog?

"You're passing through. I've seen it before. But your name..."

My real name?

"I mean, it's no thing," she said, "just as long as you're up for taking it from the top."

It hung on the tip of his tongue. Not the name the U.S. marshals had given him. His real name, one he hadn't said aloud in years.

But he didn't say it. All of a sudden he was thinking he'd broken a promise.

He'd been lying to himself. He wasn't adrift. He'd sought, he'd found.

He'd gotten far more than he deserved.

Despite the night heat, he shuddered.

He'd walked his wife into murder. His daughter scorned the thought that he'd ever existed. He was thinking that right now, right where he stood.

He looked at her. Lola. She was calling him back to bed. He withdrew, his bare feet on hardwood. He stepped on the discarded crocheted blanket.

"Whoa, J.J."

Startled by his expression, she wriggled to the bed's edge, dragging the top sheet. She worried he'd heard Joe Blunt's footsteps, the turn of a key.

"What's going on, J.J.?"

He went for his jeans.

Back at his room, he retrieved his kit bag, hidden high on a closet shelf, the Glock 17 inside.

Forty-five minutes later, he was at the station on the other side of GE Patterson. A train heading north pulled out at 10:40 p.m. He'd told the ticket seller his name was John Bleak. He paid cash.

"John Bleak," he said aloud as he splashed his face with tepid water in the train's tiny washroom.

The Hollywood Reporter story about his daughter's movie was in his wallet.

The fridge a wasteland, and the thought of shopping about as appealing as a stubbed toe, Ginger Stillwell stopped for lunch at the biker bar, the selfsame place she met that damned J.J. Walk; they sat right over there, the two of them. She ordered a grilled cheese plus bacon on whole-wheat toast and thought maybe she'd have a beer. A dusty circular saw shared a table with a couple of Mexicans with sawdust in their cuffs and hair, the pleasing scent of fresh-cut wood about them. Otherwise, she was surrounded by empty, the bikers off on some aimless caravan through red rock.

Seizing the tranquility, she closed her eyes, inhaled and then exhaled long and slow.

And then Boone came in.

"I went to your place," he said as he dropped a cheek on the stool next door.

"I'm not there."

She looked at him through the mirror behind the liquor bottles. His face was less swollen, more yellow, and the blood around the stitches had dried into tiny knobs. Knowing Boone, he was either going to keep them in his skin until they dried to ash and fell out or he would pluck them out with his fingers out of boredom.

"If I was you, I'd sit down because I'm about to rattle your brain."

She was already seated. The grilled cheese plus bacon arrived.

"You touch that, Boone, and I'm stabbing."

He glanced at the plastic fork.

Ginger wore a peasant blouse, jeans that were torn at the knees and ankle-high moccasins with fringe, no makeup. Boone's water company shirt was open and untucked; underneath, one of several Johnny Cash T-shirts he owned, this one he'd bought used, the singer's face about faded away. Ginger recognized his bucking bronc belt buckle—she'd given it to him as a gift for their lone Christmas as man and wife.

She lifted half the sandwich and pushed the rest toward him.

He gave it a long look. He and the crew had split a pepperoni pizza in the lunchroom; he grabbed the last dried-out and curled slice, which ought to explain his little bit of a stomachache, the stitch in his side. "No thanks."

"Then if you don't mind," she said, "I'd like to enjoy my own time."

"I'll make it quick." He dug into the back pocket of his jeans and withdrew a slip of paper bearing the county water company logo. "Your friend J.J. Walk."

Ginger stopped, the goopy sandwich suspended halfway to her mouth.

"He lives in Toronto, Indiana, and before you ask, yeah, there's a Toronto in Indiana."

"How did—"

He held up a finger and cleared his throat. "As I was saying: Toronto, Indiana. He returned the car at the airport in Memphis."

"He lives in Indiana," she said in wonder. She put down the sandwich without taking a bite, recalling she'd pegged him for Northern California.

"Or maybe he don't. Because the rental car people, they found out his credit card was counterfeit. Totally fake."

She grimaced in disappointment. She had him down for a good man.

Stillwell said nothing. There was no sense in telling her Walk went up to the rental car desk at the airport, asked for a manager, told her his card was no good and handed her an envelope with $590 inside.

"Boone, you aren't any closer to him than you were before."

He tugged a sliver of fatty bacon away from the sticky cheese and bit it for the taste. "How do you figure?"

"Well, where is he?"

"I'm working on that."

"With who?"

Sixty-seven-year-old Vernon Sevcik, retired Clarksdale PD, was a drinking buddy of Stillwell's late father. To get the license and rental car company, Sevcik called the county and whipped up a tale about the Cali Kia smacking his Dodge Side Step in a Taco Bell lot. Then he phoned the company, puffing himself with authority and dusting off his cop-speak. It worked. But as far as whether J.J. Walk hopped a flight? With the TSA and Homeland Security these days, bluster wouldn't play.

"Never mind who," Stillwell said to his ex-wife. "Me. That's all you need to know."

Finally, Ginger took a bite of her sandwich. Still warm. Pretty damned good too.

"Impressed?"

"I'm a little surprised you stuck with it. And you moved along further than I thought you would."

"You always underestimated me."

"No, I'm thinking I got you about right," she said as she chewed.

"I'm taking a few days vacation and heading out," he said as he slid off the stool. "I'm about to find his ass."

"Let it go," she said. She sipped from the longneck. When she returned it to the bar, a beer bubble rested on top. "He's not worth it."

"For you, no. For me, different story."

"God almighty, Boone. Can't you see? He's a pro. A flimflam man. I'm lucky he didn't steal my purse."

"Maybe there's reward."

"Boone—"

He reached and pinched her earlobe—which she hated—then stole another piece of bacon. "I'll send a postcard."

A bounce in his step, Boone Stillwell hurried out to the van, shading his eyes from the late-afternoon sun. He owed the water company four more hours and Vern Sevcik a case of brews and not the light shit neither.

Cotillion Ketchum, who worked the four-to-midnight shift at the Restful, stole some time after the dinner rush, such as it was, to do her homework on her laptop computer. She attended Yavapai Community College, majoring in small business enterprise. Her ambition was to open a modeling agency for her people, not just Yavapai-Apaches. She figured the beauty of the young girls on the res, with their regal bearing, high cheekbones and dark hair shining like ravens' wings, could serve as their ticket to mainstream opportunity. The idea was so rich, so obviously right for the times, that she' d told no one about it. Her counselor at school thought she wanted to own a Subway franchise.

"Cotillion? Excuse me."

Cotillion was sitting under a rack of hanging pots and pans, her laptop and textbooks on stainless steel. A couple of turkeys and a honey ham roasted in the ovens, the heat dispatching the autumn chill. In the doorway, a busboy was stealing a smoke before he dove elbow deep into murky dishwater.

She looked at the clock in the corner of her screen.

"You're early," she said. "Way early."

Ginger Stillwell said, "Cotillion, I was wondering if you wouldn't mind if I use your computer for a few minutes. I'll take the last hour of your shift if you want." She was already in uniform.

"Deal," Cotillion said. "If you go see if anybody needs a refill or whatever, I'll finish up right quick."

Easy enough. The Restful was empty, save for the three old-timers. If they needed a fresh cup, they could serve themselves.

When Ginger returned, the seat in front of the laptop was empty and Cotillion paced with an open textbook, a yellow highlighter floating above the page.

"What's on your mind?" she asked as Ginger sat.

"I'm trying to track down somebody."

She flexed her fingers above the keyboard. The screensaver was Cotillion's two daughters dressed up as angels, appropriate as far as Ginger was concerned.

"He might have some kind of criminal record…He's a flimflam artist."

"'A flimflam artist,'" Cotillion repeated as she looked over her shoulder. "What did he flimflam?"

"We got cozy." She went on a bit, with discretion.

"And then…?"

"Nothing. He said good-bye. J.J."

"You're losing me."

"Before we got going, he about punched Boone's face off his head."

"You want to thank him?"

Ginger smiled. "I wouldn't have minded if he stuck around."

"Like that, huh?"

She described him and Cotillion nodded, thinking if he was half as fine as Ginger indicated, she would've wanted him around too. Her next attentive lover would be her first.

"Boone's got his mind made up to find him."

"The flimflam man. J.J."

"He's the one."

"Boone. Who gets lost driving to work?"

"I know." Ginger turned. "It's not so much about finding J.J. It's keeping Boone from driving up and down America. Right now, he's somewhere between Indiana and Tennessee, trying to figure which way to go."

"To find one man," Cotillion said.

"I should mention the last place he was seen was at an airport. Which means he could be anywhere, not just—"

"Indiana or Tennessee," Cotillion said, finishing the sentence. "Big ol' country though."

"Boone hasn't had a plan yet, so I don't see as he's got one now."

The busboy threw down his cigarette butt and reached for his rubber gloves.

Cotillion said, "Do you know something he doesn't?"

"J.J. Walk might be an actor. He had a Hollywood magazine in his car and there was a big circle around a story. As far as I can tell, they're making some kind of movie."

Cotillion stepped to Ginger's side and nudged her with her hip until she could reach the keyboard. "You remember the name of the magazine?"

She did. And the company behind the film. Blabberdashery, it was called.

"I'm guessing it's a comedy," Cotillion said.

"No, no. Blabberdashery's the name of the production company."

"Let's see what that gets us," Cotillion said as she began to type.

Palms moist, ambitious little Michael Koons made the short drive from his office to the Four Seasons for a last-minute lunch with Warren Judy, the producer who put together the funding for Isabel Jellico's film. Not that anyone else in Hollywood considered it Isabel's, though her treatment did have a certain naïve charm, which was natural since she wrote the book on which it's based when she was 11. It was in the machine now; her unassigned detective Nathaniel Hill could end up a two-headed giraffe, its Civil War–era New York setting changed to Pluto in the 28th century. But to promote his young client, and in hopes of raising his standing at the agency, Koons called it hers whenever diplomacy would allow.

He arrived at the restaurant to find Warren Judy had booked a table on the sunny deck rather than in the dining room. A leather tablet case under his arm, Koons wondered what a conversation in the clear light of day meant: A tranquil, transparent setting would make bad news all the more devastating.

Judy rose to shake hands. Naturally fit with sizable shoulders and a long, tapered neck, he wore a camel blazer, a pale tangerine shirt and creased jeans. Koons, a tiny man ever eager to exude optimism, was in blue—the suit a rich navy, the shirt the color of a baby boy's pajamas. He settled in under dappled sunlight.

Chit chat. This and that. Veronica's fine, said Judy, in response to Koons's query about his partner and wife. She sends regards.

You heard about Kleindienst? Metastasized. Metastasized? They give him a year, maybe. A moment's silence. Bottled water arrived. Judy's Android buzzed. The producer thought about it, then let it go to voice mail. He ordered the branzino. Too nervous to savor a meal, Koons chose the ravioli, hoping the starch would serve as ballast. Judy, a mensch who started in the business 30 years ago as a grip, asked the waiter for a California Pinot Noir. It was delicious, the raspberry note lingering. By the time the meal arrived, small talk had evaporated.

"We've got trouble, Michael," Judy said as he lifted a delicate sliver from the filet. He had broad hands; the fish fork seemed a toy in his fingers.

"How so?"

"The Saudis are nervous."

Oh shit.

"Egypt, Libya. Iraq. Iran now. It's not a good time."

"Political unrest prohibits investment and profit?"

Judy shrugged. "Who the hell knows? I'm not telling you they're out. I'm saying they're leaning."

"That would be unfortunate," Koons managed.

"Canal Plus is still in, barely," Judy said as he pursued a green olive, "and so are the Canadians. But my guys are uncomfortable."

Judy and his partners put up 11 percent.

"I can't keep it quiet much longer, Michael."

Koons calculated. Judy hadn't mentioned the lead actor, which probably meant he was still in; therefore, so was the director. Both were clients of the mega-agency where Koons worked, and no word of the Saudis' discontent had filtered to his office, which was several flights down from the rarified air enjoyed by his senior colleagues. Failure would blunt Koons's plans to move up.

Judy topped Koons's glass. "Are you hearing me? I don't want to shop it. Not yet."

"You want me to speak to Sir Bernie," Koons said, using the chairman's nickname. "But do you really want that floating around the halls?"

"Sir Bernie is the soul of discretion," Judy said hopefully.

"I need to give his secretary a reason for the meeting." Koons looked around the deck and then whispered the actor's and director's names. "The moment I get on Sir Bernie's calendar, rumors—"

Judy said, "I'll tell them we're looking for additional funding for Blabberdashery. I'll say Sir Bernie is spinning his Rolodex."

"You were talking franchise," Koons said gently.

Not that he believed it. In a land where unadulterated praise meant no thanks, spoken promises were dandelions in a hurricane.

"Keeping the project alive and independent is good for everybody, Michael. Isabel too. Help yourself here. Go and get."

Koons nodded thoughtfully. If he kept the deal together, or found new financing, the agency would profit from its take on the actor's, director's and several costars' salaries. Sir Bernie would know he had protected the agency's stakes. Credit and reward would ensue. Even if his promotion were delayed, he would profit from Isabel Jellico's association with the promise of an ongoing enterprise, though she was already paid up front with no back-end money. Judy and his partners, including the agency, owned her characters. Sir Bernie might be persuaded to let some of that income flow toward the man who had structured the deal.

"So you've got the French—barely—the Canadians, your eleven percent," Koons counted. "How much are we talking about?"

Judy spun his Android, tapped an app and showed Koons the shortfall if the Saudis withdrew.

"I didn't realize," the agent said. The Saudis were fronting almost half the projected costs.

"I'm due in Riyadh next Tuesday," Judy said as he retrieved his device. "Those sons of bitches want to give it to me to my face. Jesus, I hate that."

4

Francis Cherry was seated on a bench in Battery Park, marveling at the long line snaking to the ferry to Ellis Island, the old immigration port. Maybe 200 people, guidebooks in every language, everybody talking to each other, overcoming Babel with hand gestures, nods and smiles. Over there, dark burly Africans in colorful garb were selling wristwatches out of briefcases.

Cherry was eating popcorn for lunch. Four hours ago, he had breakfast at Jean-Georges with the CFO of India's largest company. They talked this and that, nothing of note, Cherry finding him a titanic bore, all bilge and bluster, the guy claiming he was Atlas hoisting the world economy. "Have another croissant," Cherry said, hoping a mouthful would shut him up. If he had a conscience going in, Cherry might've felt bad about what he planned to do.

Waiting for his driver off Columbus Circle, Cherry had called in a big buy order for shares of one of the company's main suppliers, which drove the price into orbit. In Mumbai, the chairman was forced to deny the firm was acquiring the supplier, but six brokers and a Bloomberg reporter, tipped by an apparatchik at the PR agency Cerasus owned, saw Cherry eating his black truffle omelet across from the animated CFO. As he was driven down Broadway, Cherry sold before the denial crossed Reuters, up 180 million rupees.

Now, in Battery Park, Goldsworthy approached. He had been summoned. He knew what was coming. He'd failed.

He'd hired operatives and sent them to hotels in Chicago and Los Angeles, cities where Bleak had done the work Cherry admired. They went to airports and rental car companies. To Chinese laundries. Nothing.

There were 210 Brooks Brothers stores in the U.S. He called seven. Finally one of the salesmen said it. "You expect me to remember one customer because he had sandy hair and a few scars?"

In no time, Goldsworthy was devoid of ideas. A life dedicated to self-indulgence and wrath had robbed him of clarity. And regardless of what liberties it'd appeared he had taken in the intelligence service, he'd been a soldier, not a leader. He followed orders. He couldn't fathom how plans came about. Lying on a hammock in the jungle, adrift in a silver haze, he hadn't cared.

Whatever edge he'd once had was gone. Last year, on vacation at a resort on Bondi Beach in Australia, he fell asleep outside his cabana and awoke to find himself coated with lighter fluid, a young woman ready to strike a match. Turned out he'd killed her father in Ballymoney during the Troubles. Goldsworthy escaped by racing to the water and swimming to safety.

Cherry said, "You're frazzled."

He hadn't slept in days. It was a curse to be just sharp enough to recognize one's own incompetence. "No. I'm fine."

"Tall and droopy at the same time. How do you manage that?"

"All's well," he replied without conviction.

"You ever been to Ellis Island?"

"I can't say that I have, no."

"Let me ask you: How did you get into America?"

"I flew, sir."

"No, I mean, how did you get to stay?"

"A green card."

"Just like that, huh?"

Goldsworthy said, "It was arranged."

Cherry knew this. He agreed to take on Goldsworthy. A favor pays double in return. "MI6 thinks you're swell, huh?"

Not after the contretemps in Montserrat, Goldsworthy thought. The ticket to New York MI6 delivered to his prison cell was one way.

To change the subject, he said, "Sir, the CAC closed down two percent. The FTSE was up."

Cherry put his hand over his brow to block the sun. "Is that why you think you're here?"

"No, sir. I don't imagine so."

"You have John Bleak," Cherry said. "He's in the trunk of your car."

"We're closing in," Goldsworthy said.

"His real name is…"

"It's best if you don't know."

"No it's not."

"Plausible deniability, sir."

"For what? I intend to talk to him. I may do it on a float at the Thanksgiving Day Parade."

Cherry stood. The popcorn that had gathered in the folds of his suit jacket tumbled to the pathway. Plump pigeons and black squirrels hurried over.

"We'll close this out," Goldsworthy said. "It's taking longer than I thought it would. I'll grant you that. But trust me on this, sir. He will be found."

Francis Cherry looked down at his shoes. Today, he wore cap-toe oxfords he bought at Payless for 32 bucks. The black-and-gold alpaca socks were handmade and cost $480. "Trust me" was a synonym for "I'm fucking you."

He raised an eyebrow and stared at Goldsworthy. "See that ferry over there?" He pointed to the harbor. A white double-deck vessel was easing toward port. "I want you on it. Go see the Statue of Liberty, throw in with the huddled masses. Climb all the way up and stare down at the golden door."

"I don't understand."

"You're going to want to remember it. You know, when you're back in England, sweeping chimneys or frying chips or whatever the fuck you're qualified to do."

Though he knew it was coming, Goldsworthy was stunned. The ramifications were endless, as was his paranoia. MI6 was everywhere in the States; not even the NSA knew how many British intelligence agents were about. Without Cherry's protection, he'd be dead before he packed his bags.

Fighting panic, he said, "When you needed data on the airline merger, you said I was invaluable."

"Hoo-boy. Are you the only Brit I know? Don't be desperate, mate. Exit with grace."

"You can't deny—"

"I took you in and kept you straight. So what?"

"What would the Securities and Exchange—"

"Oh please."

With more force than he intended, Goldsworthy said, "I will find him, sir."

"No you won't."

"I will. I don't understand why you fail to see it."

Cherry handed Goldsworthy the red-and-white-striped cone that held his popcorn lunch. "I had one request: Find John Bleak."

Goldsworthy sighed. "There is no John Bleak."

"Is too."

Goldsworthy said, "I'll handle it, sir."

"I think you had your shot."

The drive to Memphis took 23 hours and Boone Stillwell arrived sicker than he'd ever been in his natural-born life. In Albuquerque, the pain in his stomach turned from annoying to agony. No matter how high he turned up the AC, he sweated, his black Johnny Cash-exiting-Folsom T-shirt as damp as a dishrag, even the little patch of hair under his lip dripping. Confusion set in; he thought he saw the tattoos melt on his arms. Then diarrhea struck outside Oklahoma City. He vomited out the window as he drove through Arkansas. Prayer commenced as the Tennessee state line approached.

He wondered how that son of a bitch managed to slip poison on the mug before he crashed it into his face.

Much of his coin going to overpriced convenience store drugs, Stillwell drank a bottle of Pepto-Bismol to wash down three generic Tylenol. Dizzy with pain, he stared at the double yellow line on the blacktop; concentrating the best he could manage, he made his way toward the airport. Surely somebody behind the counter at the rental car drop would remember the man who gave up $590 in cash to pay off a vehicle he could have kept, and not a screaming soul in hell would've known he'd took it. The way he chatted up Ginger—maybe he told the rental car manager where he was going, chatting her up too. Or maybe he decided to stick around Memphis, a city where Boone hadn't ever been but he'd always wanted to visit, seeing as Johnny Cash recorded at Sun Studio "I Walk the Line," "Big River," "I Forgot to Remember to Forget" and all. If he stayed, he was bound to run into him—J.J. Walk, that is, not Johnny Cash, who died in 2003, the twelfth of September, which, the hand of God at play, was Boone Stillwell's birthday. He decided he'd find a bar near Sun Studio and toast the Man in Black.

Instead, he ended up in Methodist University Hospital.

In the emergency room, a doctor entered with an X-ray in hand.

"Mr. Stillwell, you have appendicitis," said the doctor, who pulled the curtain until it closed, sort of. She was African-American and, Jesus, beautiful like some kind of TV being. "It's got to come out, I'm afraid."

"Why?" said Boone Stillwell. On his side on the gurney, he had his knees up by his chest. They insisted he remove his boots, though he told them he had more holes than socks.

"It could rupture, Mr. Stillwell."

"No, I'm asking why you're afraid."

"I'm not—Oh, I see. No." She had a warm smile, a good bedside manner. "It's a figure of speech."

"Well, when do you want to do this thing?"

"Right away. Now."

"Hold on—" But the moment he tried to turn on his side, he felt a searing jolt in his stomach. He moaned and moaned again.

"We're going to admit you and get you right upstairs."

"I've got to call somebody."

"That's all right. Just don't be planning on going anywhere."

She'd been trying to get someone in Hollywood, California, to admit there was such a production company as Blabberdashery. Finally, an extra-thoughtful 888 operator explained how these sub-sub-subshells are formed to provide a tax shelter for the bigger firms. "Didn't you ever notice all those logos that come up on the screen before the film actually starts?" the operator asked. Ginger said yes. Yes, she did. "That's just how it works. It's a form of protection, legal-wise."

Apparently, there was no possibility that she could get in touch with the director, the actors or the costars who were involved. She tried to contact the screenwriter, Isabel Jellico, but no luck there either. They hadn't failed completely, though: Cotillion found a story on the Web that explained Jellico was a teenager when she wrote the movie.

"Don't you wish you had that kind of luck?" Ginger asked, her shift about to commence at the Restful.

"Luck doesn't have much to do with it," Cotillion replied as she sent the laptop to sleep. "But now we have her agent's name. We could try us that route. I mean, if you're still up for it."

"I am. Frankly, I'm reconsidering whether J.J. actually did play me cheap. It was fine while it lasted. All my grievances are after the fact. If Boone hadn't butted in, who knows where I' d be. Right?"

Cotillion smiled. "Sure. Right."

Ginger said, "It's depressing to think what you have to go through to grab a man worth keeping."

Midnight and 1 o'clock both came and then went. Stars dotted the indigo sky. Walking the diner's empty aisle after delivering bowls of vegetable soup and crackers to its lone customers, a Canadian couple on their way to Tucson, Ginger looked up to find Johnny Eagle flagging her down with a wet towel.

In the kitchen, the dirty beige telephone handset dangled and spun above the floor. She picked it up, said hi.

"Gin, why don't you answer—"

Oh great. "Because, Boone, I—"

"I called your cell at least twenty-five times, Ginger—"

"Because I've decided that you're a fool intent on embarrassing me daily until the day I die. OK, Boone? That clear enough for you? And now I hope to heaven you're on your way home from wherever you are."

"I'm in the hospital," he said. "They're prepping me up for surgery."

She sprung to rail straight. "What? No way."

"I'm in Memphis in the damned hospital."

She had to admit he did sound a bit flustered, which, given his usual bravado, he hardly ever did.

Anger fleeing, she leaned against a table, the wall phone cord stretched and uncoiled. "What happened?"

"My appendix is set to burst."

She ran through her memory for a look at his sinewy frame. Nope. No appendix scar. "Well, good they caught it in time."

"You're coming to help me. Right, Ginger?"

"I am not."

"Ginger, baby, ain't that right? You're coming—"

"If you hadn't gone off like the imbecile you are, Boone, you could've had your appendix clipped out right here in your hometown."

He sighed. Even before he'd made it across New Mexico, Boone Stillwell realized he was on a fool's errand. All things being equal, he'd have just as soon returned home, told his friends what he'd learned about J.J. Walk, made some noise about a stolen rental car, et cetera and so forth, and said the guy run off, too chicken-ass for round two. Elbows on the bar, he would've squinted his eyes and, looking dead ahead, said something like, "Besides, he wants me, he knows where I'm at…"

"Ah, for shit's sake, Ginger. Give me a break, will you? This damned surgery could go either way."

"And I'm truly sorry for you," she said as she paced, the cord tangling behind her. "But I've got to get back to work."

"I'm doing this for you, Ginger," he shouted.

"Like hell you are."

She slammed the handset into its cradle.

The cook was watching. Johnny Eagle had wild, untamed eyebrows, a thick neck wider than his head and also bandages on every finger of his left hand. A wonder who could deep-fry beer if you wanted him to, Johnny Eagle was given to daydreaming while he carved meat, and one of these days he was going to slice off his hand at the wrist. He said, "I didn't know you were married, Ginger."

"In fact, you know I'm not."

"Didn't sound like that to me," he said, pointing toward the phone with a boning knife. Eagle was a marriage expert: He had two wives, having failed to divorce one before taking on the other. The three lived together over in Cornville.

"I'm just frustrated, is all."

"Marriage will do that to you."

"It's a life sentence, that's for sure."

5

He had no intention of staying in Carbondale. It was a way station to St. Louis. You had to connect by bus. When he was 11 years old, he crawled into the baggage hold of a Greyhound out of Ukiah. The driver put him out in Carson City. His father clapped him on the side of the head with the butt of his Remington rifle, raising a nasty welt. His ear rang for days.

St. Louis had a light-rail system. MetroLink, they called it. You could get on in Union Station and go either way. Toward the international airport or back across the river to Shiloh where there was an air force base. People coming and going.

But Carbondale was fine for a few days. A place where he could be alone again. He had to step back into the void. There had been too much exposure. He' d made new mistakes. What happened with the woman in Memphis? Her name was... He remembered how he panicked. He' d lost control. What control?

His wife had asked, "What do you want? Really. I'm not being provocative. What are you looking for?"

They were looking to patch it up. He'd gone wrong and he knew it. But she wanted to share the blame. That was her way.

"Moira," he replied, "everything I could ever want, it's here with you and Pup."

She nodded. "A family."

Yes, a family. Comfort.

"And me? Am I all you could ever want?"

Now in west Illinois, he settled in a chain motel about a mile from a college campus. Fifty-nine dollars a night and they took cash. He stared at the water stains in the ceiling, stared at the cracks in the walls. He said his name was John Bleak. J.J. Walk of Toronto, Indiana, had to go.

The woman in Memphis. Her name was Lola.

He wandered a shopping mall, the scent of bakery cinnamon trailing him. He bought a couple of paperbacks, a pair of jeans. Halloween was coming, and he noticed they were selling candy corn and stuffed animals with witches' hats and broomsticks. The greeting cards said *Boo!*

A barber shaved him with a straight edge. When the hot towel covered his face, he saw Moira. Coated in blood, her flesh shredded by fourpenny nails that studded the bomb.

He walked along Highway 51 again, and soon he was on campus under fire-orange leaves. They rippled in the evening breeze. A lake, and it rippled too. Lights in the classroom windows, in the redbrick dorms. Kids walked by him. To ward off the chill, John Bleak turned up the collar on his blue blazer and buried his hands in his pockets. He went to town and found a newsstand. He bought a copy of the latest edition of *The Hollywood Reporter* and brought it to a bar.

"What's good?" he said to the waitress.

"To tell you the truth, mister, nothing. I'd stick to the basics."

She was Pup's age, and he could tell she needed the job. She was paying her way through school. She had a plan. She was going to get out. Some people couldn't understand how far you had to go to be somewhere. He saw that she did.

A football game from the West Coast played on the TV over the bar, but it couldn't draw away the students' attention from the tabletop shuffleboard game they were playing, grainy sawdust on their hands. They slid the little metal puck back and forth, back and forth, one eye closed. There were backlit beer signs everywhere.

He ordered a turkey sandwich.

"Good choice," said the waitress.

"You have potato salad, coleslaw or something like that?" he asked.

She was a kid, he told himself. Leave her be.

"Yes, sir. We do," she replied. But she gave her head a little shake, her face a mask of horror.

"OK, the sandwich," he said, smiling in return. "And a beer."

He opened the magazine.

Boone Stillwell was surprised to learn a man dreams when he's under general anesthesia. He was equally surprised, probably more so, to find out that they kick you out of the hospital after the operation. Don't matter how much you ache and moan.

"Make sure you walk for exercise," said the nurse's aide as she rolled him down the corridor toward the exit, rubber tires squeaking and squealing. "Take it slow and easy, but walk as much as you can. Keep at it."

Maybe I ought to walk my bony ass back home, he thought, seeing as you told me I shouldn't drive while I'm taking these pain pills. But he kept his yap shut. He was feeling pretty much a moron since he woke up in recovery. He couldn't exactly remember his dream, but it had something to do with Ginger in a wedding gown telling him he was God's greatest mistake.

What a dope, chasing a stranger across a bunch of states, and to do what? Shoot him? A) Boone shot at cactus for target practice and he ain't hit one yet from more than 10 feet out, and 2) He couldn't shoot a man even if he had the aim. He was no street-fighting man. He had no idea why he pulled that sap back in Jerome, which he carried for good luck and it brought him none.

Outside the hospital, families gathered to retrieve their loved ones, cars waiting with open doors, grandkids holding balloons. His clothes smelled of sickness and the physical indignities he suffered on the drive east.

"Here you go, Mr. Studwell," the nurse said as she pulled the chair's brake.

"Stillwell." He groaned to upright. "You know, these painkillers don't do much good."

She tapped him once on the back. "Good luck."

Thinking if he was a kid at least they would've gave him a lollipop, Boone Stillwell limped to his car, where his pearl-handle pistol lay buried in his toolbox.

Mrs. Brent's tiny assistant froze at the sight of Francis Cherry entering the office at 6 a.m., the lights off, the coffee yet to percolate, copies of *The Wall Street Journal* in a pile in the hall. Coat on, she was still wearing her earbuds, hip-hop's relentless pulse having kept her from falling back to sleep on the long subway ride from north of Yankee Stadium down to Wall Street.

"You," Cherry said as he approached her desk. "We're moving fast today. Go find Mrs. Brent."

She flicked the buds from her ears, and the hissing beat found Cherry. Her eyes burst wide in horror. No one knew his rules, but she was certain she'd offended one.

"I'm sorry, Mr. Cherry." Trembling, she fumbled for the player. The Bronx was a battleground, no doubt, and ready training. But this was Francis Cherry. Congressmen groveled.

"What's your name?" he asked.

"I have three kids," she replied.

Oy. Cherry had no time for bullshit. He was energized, his neurons firing solid-gold synapses since he cut Goldsworthy loose. The woman quivering over there was wasting his time.

But Legal had warned him. One of these days, a chewed-up admin was going to reject a settlement and go to the *Post*. Cherry committed to change, but he'd lasted four minutes with the anger management whiz.

"Miss Three Kids," he said calmly. "Would you please find Mrs. Brent for me? I thank you."

Still quaking, she left the building, got back on the 4 train and went to Mrs. Brent's apartment on the Upper East Side. There she fainted.

Mrs. Brent appeared 28 minutes later in Cherry's office. In shirtsleeves, his tie at half-mast, he was staring at the Bloomberg terminal, seeing invisible things. Awaiting his attention, ideas and innovations hovered like hummingbirds.

She cleared her throat. She'd already made up her mind that if he insisted she fire Estelle Negron, she would resign in protest.

Cherry turned to allow the 76-year-old to read his lips.

"You wouldn't by any chance know an artist, would you?" he said. "The kind who can really, you know, draw?"

Three hours later, Cherry stepped off his private plane in Montreal with a young woman in a crocheted vest, long-sleeve T, no bra, flowing tie-dyed skirt and sandals. She smelled like violets and had her dark hair done in two very long braids. Hippie redux, Cherry thought. He regretted he could never be so free.

In the back of the stretch limousine, the woman dug into her satchel and produced an artist's tablet she balanced on her lap. A box of pastels rested on the padded seat. She faced Cherry, who needed lunch.

On the flight north, he watched a video on her cell phone—a compilation of her work as it appeared on Court TV, CNN, NBC affiliates, et cetera, the trials where you can't bring in cameras. She was very thorough. Gifted, even. A photographer couldn't have done much better.

"Ready?" he asked.

She nodded. Hell of a day, huh? One minute she's reusing a tea bag, the next she's on a luxury jet to Canada with the promise of $10,000 if she could produce. She usually billed at $80 a day plus subway fare and lunch.

Cherry said, "No scribbling, no composite drawing. No Identi-Kit."

She nodded again.

"What I want, when you're through, is the world thinking there's a new Rembrandt."

The tips of the fingers on her right hand were pastel rainbows. So was the meat above her wrist.

"John Bleak." Cherry began to describe a man he and Ian Goldsworthy had seen once, over lunch in Elizabeth, New Jersey, a few months ago. "He's got sandy hair—"

"The shape of the face, please," Daphne said as she raised a white charcoal.

By the time they arrived in Montreal's Plateau District, Daphne Cook-Ryerson was on her third draft. Cherry was astonished. With the heel of his shoe, he kicked himself in the shin, corporal punishment for failing to think of this sooner.

Cook-Ryerson continued to work as Cherry sopped up cheese curds and brown gravy.

"I have to say you are good, Daphne," Cherry said between bites. The poutine restaurant was stuffed with Quebecois hipsters who tried to disguise their interest in a pretty, time-traveling American woman.

She said thanks as she continued to refine the portrait.

Cherry shoveled up another mouthful. "I know what you're thinking," he said as he chewed. "Why this?"

Daphne looked up. A drop of gravy sat on Cherry's chin. "Not really."

"A job's a job, huh?"

"More or less." As she went back to her sketch pad, she said, "We're all trying to get by."

"I never did understand that," Cherry said. "In the arts the pay never equals the talent. It's either much too much or far too little with you guys."

As she rubbed a line with her ring finger, Daphne Cook-Ryerson wondered if she should tell Cherry about the gravy stain.

He watched. Look at that kid go. She gnawed her lip as she drew.

Suddenly, she sat back, lifted the pad and turned it for Cherry to see.

He was looking at John Bleak.

6

Boone Stillwell patrolled the bars on Beale Street and found J.J. Walk in exactly none. The ache below his belly was gone, the pain more or less too, and now he itched like a son of a bitch, and he was down to his last $32 and his car smelled like a fart factory.

Done kidding himself, he was killing time so he could go back home with a shred of dignity still hanging to his sorry bones.

There was no use denying it now. He was as fucked up as Ginger always said he was.

"No, I don't mean she said it out loud," he told a bartender who looked like the Chicago Cubs teddy-bear logo. "But you know when they stare at you in a certain way. Like all the disappointment in the world is coming out of you."

"Can't say that anybody looked at me like that," Mr. Cub replied with a shrug as he dried a glass.

Boone was the only customer in the bar. A single beer for breakfast had him halfway to drunk.

"Not even when you left the seat up?"

"Why would I leave the seat up?"

"Ah, go to hell," Boone said as he managed to scale off the stool.

He walked back to his car and decided to go home, but first he'd say good-bye to Johnny Cash down at Sun Studio. He drove Union Avenue with the windows open, the newspapers he'd used for blankets fluttering in the downhill breeze.

Ian Goldsworthy bought a big long canvas shoulder bag, packed up his belongings, took the $47,000 he had in cash out of his safe and flagged a taxi to LaGuardia.

Through a long, gin-soaked night, Goldsworthy came to realize if he was going to survive, he had to exploit whatever resources he could, both innate and professional. He had no choice: Having failed to finesse Cherry or conceal his own shortcomings, he had to find John Bleak, kill John Bleak and then convince Cherry to take him back. Use Cherry's line against him: "You said you feared his return, sir. No need to fear now. I did as instructed."

Slipping into covert mode, he went into the Delta terminal, walked to a kiosk and called up a flight, but he didn't buy a ticket, though it looked for all the world like he did. He hurried downstairs, stepped out into the morning light and hailed a cab to Penn Station.

Goldsworthy took Amtrak to Philadelphia and checked into the Four Seasons Hotel off the Ben Franklin. To his surprise, Cherry had yet to cancel his credit cards. He asked the concierge to look into overnight flights to Istanbul. Book me into your sister hotel near the Bosphorus, he added as sweetener.

He called Langley, tapping out the number on the phone in his suite. As if astonished, an old ghost-war buddy said, "Ian Goldsworthy. As I live and breathe. I heard you were sent to detention, pal."

Goldsworthy made his request as he unpacked his laptop.

The reply came back positive. "Sure. Send them down."

He e-mailed John Bleak's fingerprints to CIA headquarters.

Forty-two minutes later, the room phone rang.

"Guy doesn't exist," said the CIA operative.

"Impossible, mate," Goldsworthy said. He wore the white courtesy robe. "I've met him."

"He's not in the system."

"Why not?" Goldsworthy had concluded John Bleak was either a career criminal or a cop.

The operative declined to speculate. Then, speculating, he said, "He could be in WITSEC."

"Are you telling me you can't access—"

"Witness Protection is Justice. The U.S. marshals."

"And you don't talk to each other, I presume."

"Unless the president calls the heads together, no."

"What a load of bollocks."

"You, on the other hand, chum, are fire-engine red. Is there anybody in MI6 you haven't pissed off? I'm surprised you'd come back on the grid. I'm thinking you stay at the hotel and I'll—"

Goldsworthy cut the line. The CIA could look for him in Istanbul, though he had no intention of leaving the States.

He thought hard and long about what to say. He felt Pup's disappointment, though knowing her she'd already moved on. Still, he wanted to help.

The Hollywood Reporter said the Saudi cartel had backed out and the film based on Pup's novel was in jeopardy. The director already had another project in mind. No word yet from the actor, a former reprobate and two-time Oscar nominee.

He pulled the clipping out of his wallet and read it again. The wind tousled his sandy hair.

He needed the right gambit. Too subtle and he'd seem coy and insincere. Too aggressive and here's the kind of man who would capitalize on his own daughter's misfortune.

He had access to capital. Moira had left him a small fortune. He'd arranged for Pup's welfare, as Moira would've done had she left a will, but he'd kept a chunk of the proceeds from the sale of the apartment in Manhattan and the house in Dennis on the Cape. They were funding his travels. At the rate he spent, he believed he could stay lost forever.

He was outside a gas station and convenience store in Carbondale. It served as the local Greyhound depot. The bus to St. Louis would arrive in 20 minutes, he was told. The driver would sell him a ticket. The man who called himself John Bleak walked up and down the store's aisles; 300 kinds of chips for sale, but no paperback novels. There was a mini-mall up the block. No bookstore, according to the totem sign, but a Laundromat. Maybe someone left a book behind.

As he started walking, he chided himself for his poor planning. Three hours on the bus to St. Louis with nothing to read and nothing but memories to occupy his thoughts. Dumb.

He dialed Pup's agent at his home number.

Michael Koons, who was transfixed by the image on the TV in his bedroom, backpedaled to the phone on his nightstand. He wore a cream-and-orange-striped shirt from Thomas Pink, boxers and carrot socks. His slacks and jacket were on the mahogany valet in his walk-in closet.

"Michael, it's—"

"Good God, Sam. What's happening?"

As if he were talking to him in person, Koons pointed the clicker toward the TV screen.

"I read about the problems with the film," John Bleak said. "I was wondering if I could help."

"Sam," he repeated, using the name the marshals had given Isabel's dad. "Sam, are you near a TV?"

"No. Why?" The Illinois sun was high overhead. He turned to see if the bus was early.

"Sam, get to a TV."

"Michael—"

"Get to a TV, Sam."

The tour done, Boone Stillwell walked into the gift shop at Sun Studio, thinking maybe he could buy something for Ginger, I don't know, a postcard or a ballpoint pen or one of those shot glasses with the yellow Sun logo on it, which was about all he could afford.

As Stillwell hefted the shot glass in his hand, he took a glance at the TV behind the cashier's station.

The shot glass dropped to the floor.

"Holy shit. That's him," said Boone Stillwell. Suddenly animated, he jabbed a frantic finger toward the screen. "That's him. That's J.J. Walk."

The dark-haired woman who gave the tour, all snug in her jeans and black Sun T, bumped into him as she stepped toward the counter.

"Wow," Lola Styles said, "that *is* him."

"What's he done?" Stillwell asked aloud.

"Something," she replied.

A pixilated rendering of a drawing of the man's face now filled the screen. Pulsing red letters above his head asked, Do You Know This Man?

"I know him," they said in unison.

Now pulsing, also in red: Reward!

Surrounded by a jostling crowd in Times Square that overflowed the sidewalk and spilled into the streets, Francis Cherry looked up at a digital billboard and its million twinkling lights.

"Now that," he said aloud, "is one hell of an idea."

He'd paid a considerable sum to have the drawing of John Bleak made by Daphne Cook-Ryerson placed for 10 minutes on the side of a financial-service company's glass tower, the billboard the length and width of a football field. His flacks notified CNN, FOX, Televisa and the CBC, as well as the local network TV affiliates, the print media, a handful of blogs, radio even. Now John Bleak's face was careening via satellite all over North America and YouTubing around the world.

Cherry looked at his watch—a Timex Indiglo; the band was made from Louisiana pine-snake skin. The billboard would be up for another 30 seconds. Twenty-nine, 28…

He turned to squeeze his way through shoulder-to-shoulder gawkers, their heads tilted back. Tourists up Broadway and Seventh Avenue were pointing high and taking photos. They were calling their friends. All the TV cameras aimed skyward had them excited, as did the promise of an unspecified cash reward, Cherry's nod to the realities of human nature.

7

The man whose face was on a billboard in Times Square called his daughter's agent.

Bluetooth in ear, Koons was driving sunny Santa Monica Boulevard toward his office. As much as he loved Isabel Jellico, he had no time for this. Sir Bernie had agreed to a midday meeting. One on one, at least for now. The race was on to replace the Saudi money. Koons could save Isabel's franchise, but, to reduce it to an elemental reality, if he found financing before any other agent in the firm, he was certain to be invited to escape the hell of repping screenwriters.

"Sam, she knows," he repeated. Koons found her as she was about to enter the Higashi Honganji Buddhist Temple, a skateboard ride away from her place.

The voice from Carbondale said, "Get in touch with my father and tell him to call her." The brim of the St. Louis Cardinals' cap he'd bought at the convenience store cast a shadow across his face.

Koons nodded. Isabel spent last Christmas with her grandfather up at the ranch. Since the cranky old SOB hated his son, they shared a strong bond. "She's not concerned. I mean, the guy's in jail, isn't he?"

Yes. The man who killed Moira was in jail. So was the man's father, the hired gun they'd testified against.

The bus waited by the gas station, its engine puttering. The driver was operating a little lift to board a man in a wheelchair.

"Somebody is going to find her photo."

"She shut down her old Facebook page," Koons reminded him. "She—"

"Michael, I know where Pup's photos are on the Web. Search under her real name and you'll find them too."

Koons said, "Yeah, but so what?"

"Do you know her real name?"

"Do you know mine, Sam?"

"No, but—"

"The point being, it's Hollywood. It doesn't matter."

He hesitated. "It's going to stir up some dust."

Which can't hurt, Koons thought. The right buzz might have a resuscitative effect. Is that a word? *Resuscitative*? Note to self: If so, drop it on Sir Bernie.

Koons wriggled around a road crew pouring asphalt. With a free hand, he held his nose. "I understand your concern, Sam. I do. But I don't see it's an issue."

"Tell her if she goes away for a week or ten days, she'll avoid being associated with me."

In Carbondale, the bus driver waved the queue on board. He trailed, clinging to the phone, thinking of something to say that would reach his daughter. The distance between them was as vast and unbridgeable as ever.

"Keep her safe, Michael."

"I'm betting the FBI," said Ginger as she stole yet another glance at Cotillion's laptop.

Dinnertime at the Restful. A tour bus from a visit to a vineyard owned by a rock star pulled into the lot, and now Johnny Eagle was whipping up the once $6 and now $9 blue-plate special—ham steak, curry mashed potatoes and collard greens—like he was back in Perryville, cooking for convicts by the hundreds. The Restful smelled like hog heaven; Mohawk-wearing, nose-ringed tattoo-heads in logo hoodies were testifying to Eagle's culinary genius. Cotillion and Ginger agreed the thirtysomethings were beyond polite, but buying high-end wine had them tapped out. Tips would come in coins. But having fed the bus driver for free, they figured future business would come their way. That was Cotillion's idea.

"Up," shouted Eagle as four more grilled ham steaks hit plates.

Ginger scooted to slap down scoops of potatoes and greens.

"I don't think that's the FBI's style," said Cotillion, over by the swinging doors. "Billboards in Times Square."

"Just my luck," Ginger said. "A serial killer."

"He's not a serial—"

"Terrorist."

"Ginger."

Johnny Eagle clanked the spatula on the stove. "Ladies, let's hop to it." He'd given thought to calling in his wives to help out.

As the clatter of silverware and the buzz of conversation wafted toward them, Ginger filled Cotillion's cork-topped tray.

"Least now you know his name."

"I like J.J. Walk better. Had it an air of mystery."

Cotillion hoisted the tray to her shoulder. "I still say you ought to call about the reward."

"I mean, what kind of name is that?"

"Donald Harry Bliss," said Ian Goldsworthy.

"Ssssh," went the anal-retentive businessboy across the train's aisle.

Without thinking, Goldsworthy had chosen the quiet car on the Acela back toward New York. Thinking, he wished he had his Sig Sauer P238. He'd like to blow businessboy's brains all over his French cuffs, spreadsheets and onion-flavored crisps. It would be worth the leap from a moving train.

He learned of Cherry's decision to go public in the bar at the Four Seasons Hotel. As he stared at the TV screen, he understood his banishment was just about complete: I've moved on without you, Cherry was shouting. Ian Goldsworthy: You. Are. Finished.

Goldsworthy had little to offer, but it was something. On his walk to 30th Street Station, he hit Cherry's private number. No reply. When he called Mrs. Brent, he shouted as if he'd forgotten she had 80 decibels of amplification in her handset. With chilly efficiency, Mrs. Brent said she would tell Mr. Cherry he had called.

When the Acela train left Philadelphia and crossed into New Jersey, Goldsworthy went into the vestibule to try Cherry again. An automated message told him his mobile account had been canceled. He hurried to the café car; there he discovered his American Express card had been voided too.

Now the plonker across the aisle clacked away on his keyboard. People up and down the rattling car watched films or played games on their laptops and tablets, and Goldsworthy powered on to use the free wireless to learn what everyone in the U.S., Canada and Mexico was saying about Donald Harry Bliss. So far, not a word about WITSEC, but news gathered quickly. Checking media sites and TMZ, Goldsworthy discovered Bliss had testified at a mob trial. His wife had been killed.

He disappeared. The U.S. marshals declined comment, silently verifying they'd hidden him and that he'd gotten away.

In Goldsworthy's mind, a plan began to set. Media aside, all the buzz on the Web was about the reward. It was only a matter of time before someone spotted Donald Harry Bliss, pointed a little video camera at him, posted it online and indicated where he was. Bliss would try to hide, but a trail would exist. It seemed he wasn't trained in law enforcement or espionage. Turns out Bliss was an amateur.

Goldsworthy reasoned that the marshals could've found him easily enough, Donnie Bliss/John Bleak in plain sight in Chicago and LA during the past few months. Which meant they didn't want him back. Nothing was standing in Goldsworthy's way.

The conductor announced the next station stop as Newark, causing the businessboy to tsk at the disturbance. Goldsworthy shut down his laptop and stood to gather his belongings. He swung his laptop bag so that it knocked a can of fizzy pop all over his neighbor's tray.

Goldsworthy stared down at him, eager for a challenge. The man's head, he calculated, would crack the safety window but not quite go all the way through. Had he the time, he'd stuff him in the overhead bin. For a moment, he felt an old rush, the stirring of history. Maybe the drugs and ennui hadn't killed his testosterone and adrenalin pumps after all.

"You—You did that on purpose," the man sputtered.

"Ssssh," replied Goldsworthy, a long finger across his lips.

"I will not—"

Goldsworthy broke his nose with the flat of his hand.

He was deep into Newark Penn Station before the police arrived.

Sitting two rows behind the rear exit, Donnie Bliss pulled down the Cardinals' cap brim, folded his arms and nestled against the sidewall. No one would question why he was covering his face. A man who sleeps on a bus covers his face. He blocks the sun.

He would make it to St. Louis. A quick run to the wrong side of town. A flophouse where he could lay low until he could cobble together a plan.

He wondered who wanted him.

The man who swore he'd kill him, the same man who'd killed his wife, would never resort to a thing so melodramatic as a billboard in Times Square to manipulate media. He lacked the wit for it. That man was a plodding beast. A psychopath. He had no friends. No allies, at least none Manfredi and the marshals identified.

If not him, who?

A few months ago, Bliss was tangled in an incident that resulted in the death of three violent men. No one was left alive who might come after him.

But the person who had funded them might.

Why? Bliss had returned what was taken from Francis Cherry, who claimed he was satisfied. Cherry had given his word.

A Wall Street dealmaker had given his word.

Donnie Bliss shifted in his seat as the bus stopped in Du Quoin. Passengers off, passengers on. The ones coming on might've seen his photo before they left their homes.

8

In his black nylon jacket, fire-spewing dragon on its back, Joe Blunt was sitting in a rocking chair, his bamboo knitting needles clacking together. The chair squeaked, his boots squeaked, the brokedown bar otherwise deadly quiet save for the sound of a moist beer glass as it returned to hardwood.

Sun rays through the dust-coated window, plus the bright lamp above the pool table, shed ample light on Joe Blunt's hands and wrists. He was making a sweater for Tooley's sister, who was closing on her GED; not an easy pattern, flowers culled from the Grateful Dead's Skull & Roses logo on the shoulder, but Joe Blunt was a knitting son of a bitch. Crochet too, skills he picked up in Brushy, where he did a stretch for killing a rival oxy dealer, though not before stealing his cash and stash. Inconceivable the state would give Joe Blunt weapons like knitting needles and crochet hooks to work with, but he appreciated the trust and not once did he jab one through anyone's eye. Though he did use a ball of yarn to stop his cellmate from snoring, shoving it in deep and an inch short of permanent.

Joe Blunt had dark hair thinned to a widow's peak, a perpetual five-o'clock shadow and a deadly glare. Broad across the shoulders and toned, he had developed a paunch: When he worked legit, he trucked, and when he wasn't working, he was in his rocking chair, needles click-clacking, yarn rising from a frayed Sun Studio tote. Still a formidable presence, though. Now and again, he picked up a few bucks on the side as a bouncer at the bars and clubs on Beale Street, wearing earplugs to save him from suffering third-rate jump blues. Dealing oxy, transporting oxy was part of the picture too.

"Joe Blunt," shouted the mousy bartender. "Phone."

Assorted patrons jumped. Then they turned slowly to gauge Joe Blunt's reaction.

Lost in numbing concentration, Joe Blunt hadn't stirred.

Clack clack, went the bamboo needles.

"Joe Blunt," she yelled again.

Squeak, went the rocking chair. Squeak, went his boots.

"Er, uh, Joe Blunt…" said the man nearest to the pool table. His skeleton frame was lost inside an old shirt he'd worn at a filling station a long while ago. "Excuse me."

If Joe Blunt snapped out wrong, the only question was whether he'd crack the man in half now or shove him into his T-shirt pocket to deal with later.

"Joe Blunt. The goddamned phone," the bartender bellowed. "It's Lola."

Joe Blunt looked up.

"Lola," whispered the man at the bar, an uncomfortable grin on his worn and wrinkled face.

Joe Blunt rested his needles and yarn on the pool table. The chair groaned as he stood. His boots squeaked as he strode toward the phone.

Boone Stillwell was all sorts of pumped up. "What I'm saying is we ought to pool our resources. Two heads and shit. Right? Right?"

"I don't know..." said Lola Styles, fist on hip as they continued their discussion in the late-afternoon sunlight outside the tourist trap. She was buying time.

"You know shit. I know shit. Come on." Stillwell stuck out his hand. "Fifty-fifty on any and all rewards. Come on."

She looked at him. The man who could not shut up was bobbing and ducking in place like a little boy on Christmas morning. "All right. Sure," Lola Styles said, "fifty-fifty."

She gave him directions on how to get from Sun Studio to her place over by the river. "Give me an hour or so to clean it up," she said with a wave as he walked toward his Arizona plates.

The sun set over Wall Street, and in his office Francis Cherry was filled with the warmth of well-being. Nobody knew what he was up to. Wait. Wait a minute. Hoo-boy. How great would that look on a tombstone: Francis Cherry. Nobody Knew What He Was Up To.

"Oh, I am on fire today," Francis Cherry said to the little red-ear turtle he bought in Times Square. Someone had painted the Twin Towers on its shell. Cherry didn't approve. Even a $2 turtle deserved its dignity.

Slipping into the double-breasted jacket of his gray pin-striped suit, he summoned Mrs. Brent and turned so she could read his lips.

"Go to Capital Markets and bring me the most impressive guy you can find."

She returned with Koo Young-Soon. He was at least six-and-a-half feet tall and well built, with sleepy eyes behind a broad, flat face. Cherry saw a man who appeared both sluggish and a threat.

"You are implacable," Cherry said as he came from behind the desk. The CEO of Brazil's largest petrochemical company was waiting in an adjacent conference room.

"Thank you," Mr. Koo replied, his voice rumbling with bass tones. He had his hands clasped behind his back, his legs apart. A regular Beefeater, this one.

"Home run, Mrs. Brent." Cherry rubbed his palms together. "A gold star on your permanent record."

"Very well," she replied, a chill in her voice. The memory of Estelle Negron fainting in her doorway still upset her.

"By the way, tell your peppy little assistant—Negron?—that each of her kids gets a share of Berkshire Hathaway Class A on his 21st birthday if they're in college." The stock opened at $120,000 per share. The price of peace.

Tramping a 200-year-old Persian silk rug, Cherry led Koo across his office to a pair of bloated leather sofas and sat with his back to Broad Street. Koo noticed on the oak coffee table a folio from Homeland Security marked Classified. Also a turtle.

"So here's the deal. The name Donald Harry Bliss: How many bells does it ring?"

"Zero," Koo replied.

"I thought you' d say 'none.'"

"None is not a number, sir."

Forty-two thousand calls had been received so far by the 888 number Cherry had his flacks set up at Telephonic Data Exchange. Operators in a boiler room listening to voice recordings were cataloguing information. The call from Donald Harry Bliss was the only one that mattered, and it wasn't going to come through the reward line. But what the hell, thought Cherry, let's collect puzzle pieces and see if they fit. You never know what might have value. Also let's see how low people will stoop for a reward.

To Koo, Cherry explained: Donald Harry Bliss—and until a few hours ago, I thought his name was Bleak, John Bleak—is some sort of heroic tragic figure. They killed his wife. He declined the protection of the U.S. marshals. I don't know, but it looks like he decided to go into the personal-protection business maybe. A professional Samaritan. He used to live here, but now he's out there.

Cherry raised his arm and flicked his fingers toward the great elsewhere.

"Am I clear?"

The strapping Korean nodded once.

"What I would like from you is a piece of information about Donald Harry Bliss that is spectacularly useful. Can you tell me why?"

"You want the man to return to New York."

"And what's going to make him do that?"

"A fact."

"A fact you wouldn't believe."

"By its nature, a fact is beyond dispute."

"Don't get clever on me, Koo."

Koo looked to his lap.

"I know what you're thinking," Cherry said. "Why me?"

Koo Young-Soon continued to stare at his folded hands.

"Every now and then, luck. Don't overthink it. Take it for what it's worth."

Finally, Koo raised his eyes. He thought he should tell Cherry that he'd majored in finance at NYU. He was devoted to role-playing video games. Whatever Cherry had been told about his abilities was in error.

"So?" Cherry said. He dipped his fingers into his jacket pocket, broke off a tiny sliver of lettuce and put it within easy reach of the turtle, who began its slow crawl toward its meal. "You ready, Mr. Koo?"

Koo blinked.

Incredible, Cherry thought as they stood, the sofas wheezing. The guy's perfect. He can't say no. He could be worth keeping, even after Bliss settles in.

Lola Styles laid out some leftover fried chicken and coleslaw, Stillwell confessing to being hungry and next to broke. She figured if she could get him to calm down and eat, she might be able to prime him for exactly what he knew. Still in her black Sun Studio T-shirt, she joined him at the little table by the sink, yellow pad and pencil at her elbow.

Earlier, Stillwell felt the need to show her his new scar and stitches, pulling down the band of his Iron Man Underoos. Now, he spun his chair around, its back touching the table. He straddled it and lowered himself to the seat.

The fried chicken looked damned good. But he was focused. Eating could wait.

"Now I think we agree he was out by me first," he said as he sipped a cold beer.

"You said California." She'd pulled back her midnight hair and set it in place with one of those plastic horseshoe-looking things.

"I mean, he came from California. After we went toe-to-toe, he left quick and came here by car. But now he's gone."

"Gone to where?" she asked, sneaking a glance at the clock.

"That's an issue. What did he tell you?"

She shook her head as she reached a fork toward reheated mac and cheese. "You first. We agreed, remember?"

She didn't want to say it, but she figured if he was still in Memphis, she would've seen him again. No matter what Joe Blunt said to damage her self-regard, she knew men just didn't leave her bed without wanting to return.

"I wonder if maybe he told Ginger where he was coming from."

He'd given Lola Styles the whole story—the flirting right out in public, the sucker punch, Stillwell's minor detective work that led him to the road. Maybe he'd even admitted he was out here because he was eager for Ginger to restore him to good esteem.

"Ginger, she has a memory for detail."

"Now you're saying it's a three-way split?"

Stillwell calculated. "No, I'll cover her end." He'd already had the reward money spent: a 46-inch LCD HDTV with Blu-ray in a little house with a garden for Ginger in back and a jukebox for his living room that played whatever he wanted at the snap of his finger. Also, he thought he'd buy the Restful for Ginger too. Why the hell not?

He lifted a chicken drumstick and ripped into a bite. Cheek packed, he said, "I wonder if Toronto, Indiana, means anything."

As headlights swept into the alley behind the house, Lola Styles made another note. Earlier, she said she hadn't known there was a Toronto in Indiana.

"Did he have a car when you met?"

"No, I drove him over." She glanced sideways toward the darkness beyond the adjacent living room.

"So let's say he stuck around without a car. Then what? He walked back to the airport? Took a taxi? Hitched? When he could've just left before?"

You know, Memphis has its appeal, she thought. But she let it go. Stillwell more than likely had it right: Donald Harry Bliss took himself either a Greyhound bus or an Amtrak train to leave town. To where was an issue, though not quite yet.

She said, "Why don't you call her? Your Ginger."

He put down the now-empty beer bottle and unsaddled himself from the chair. "I'll give it another try," he said. His phone was charging in the bathroom.

She started to gather up the dishes. "I hope you don't take this the wrong way. But if you'd like to use the shower, by all means."

Stillwell looked down at his wrinkled clothes, half-expecting to find Johnny Cash holding his nose. "Piss-poor planning."

"No big thing," she said as she clattered the dishes in the sink.

He pulled off his boots as he hopped, one leg, then the other, toward the bathroom.

Soon, Boone Stillwell was in an old claw-foot tub under a cascade of hot water, his first shower since he left Arizona. As steam mounted inside the curtain, he leaned his palms against the cracked tile, growing more relaxed by the second, his body ahhhing in pleasure. Spirit lifted, he was thinking maybe by the time he was through washing, Ginger would return his calls.

"Come on, Ginger," he'd said to her voice mailbox, ringing her on his ride west away from Sun Studio. "Don't you know what's happening? This is the ticket. The ticket."

He soaped up good, careful to avoid scratching the stitches below his belly button, hand on the windowsill for balance.

"Ginger, now you listen. I am telling you we have got to move on this thing. What we have is real, legitimate information."

He chose the dandruff shampoo from the windowsill.

If it all went according to plan, he'd take down whatever Lola Styles recalled, they'd ring that 888 number and, before you knew it, they'd be on a plane to New York City. Lola would have to front him for some new clothes in the morning, but she better than anybody would know he was good for it. Hell, they were likely to be splitting more money than Lola knew what to do with.

Whipping up a lather on his head, Boone Stillwell wondered if he would be better to have Ginger join him in New York City or for her to see him beaming all over the planet on TV. She just might—

A thunderous punch struck Stillwell in the temple and he flew against the shower sidewall, his head cracking against tile. Stunned, he struggled to stay upright but couldn't balance in the soapy tub. He grabbed at the curtain, and as he fell hard on his back, it snapped off its hooks.

An angry big man with a widow's peak and a scruff on his cheeks and chin reached down and held Stillwell by the jaw. He had a prison tat that began on the top of his hand and crossed his knuckles. A five-point star.

"What did she tell you?" he said.

"I don't—" The streaming water made it impossible for Stillwell to speak. He' d slid down toward the drain.

Joe Blunt lifted him and then punched him square in the face, another crushing blow. Blood flowed from Stillwell's nose.

"What did your girl tell you?"

"She's my wife," Stillwell managed, his mouth full of blood.

His T-shirt and skin slick with water, the big man reared back and struck him again. Stillwell's head bounced on cast iron.

"Joe," said Lola Styles. "He didn't get hold of her." She had Stillwell's phone in her hand. "No call is more than a half-minute long."

Now Blunt stepped over the bathtub wall and dropped his boot on Stillwell's chest. "California. Arizona. Memphis," he said.

"Right."

"Which city in California?"

"I don't know," he said, spitting bloody water. "He had California plates."

Joe Blunt demanded the license number.

Stillwell replied as best he could.

"The company. The rental company."

He told him.

"What city in Arizona?"

Stillwell coughed. Blood sprayed.

Now Joe Blunt shifted his weight until he was standing with one foot pressing down on Stillwell's chest, the other in the air.

Stillwell groaned in pain as his skinny legs rose.

Joe Blunt said, "What else you got?"

Blood backing down his throat, Stillwell tried to speak but couldn't.

"I said, what else you got?"

"Let him up, Joe," Styles said. "He's a kid."

Joe Blunt looked down at Stillwell, bloody, bruised and naked in the gathering water.

"Joe..." she said as she drew nearer.

Joe Blunt jutted his hand through the showering water, clamped on Stillwell's throat and hoisted him up and out of the tub.

Sopped and dripping, Stillwell trembled as he steadied himself on the bath mat. Scrawny as a newly hatched bird, he reached out for the towel rack, certain he was ready to fall.

Joe Blunt spun to leave, Lola Styles stepping aside.

Through the haze, Stillwell looked at his phone, thinking, Jesus, Ginger, help me, baby. Please.

Suddenly, Joe Blunt returned. With a bestial yowl, he hit Stillwell with a monstrous right hand to the center of his face.

Stillwell fell back into the tub and banged his head against the point of the windowsill. He collapsed instantly, hitting the tub floor with a clang and a dull thud.

Lola Styles struggled to pass her boyfriend.

She saw Stillwell's blood mingle with water.

As she reached in to lift him, she shouted, "Joe, you killed him. You killed him, Joe."

Joe Blunt kept walking, his rage over Lola's night with this Donald Harry Bliss not quite spent.

9

Joe Blunt bleached his clothes in the kitchen sink while they rehearsed their scheme. Glowering naked, his body marred with scars from childhood cigarette burns and amateur ink, he turned and told her to go ahead. Retreating to the bedroom, she called the 888 number. Stillwell's body was in the tub, his blood still oozing.

"Hello," Lola Styles said. Dutiful-like, she gave her name and number, and she said, "This man on TV? Donald Harry Bliss? I saw him here in Memphis. Memphis, Tennessee. He said he came east from Arizona. I had a couple of drinks with him."

Joe Blunt stared at her.

"Then next I saw him hassling this kid out on Beale Street. On Third Street, actually. He had a car with Arizona plates, this kid. He had a soul patch and a Johnny Cash T. I don't know if they had a fight or whatever. I just left. I just got out of there. That man Bliss seemed angry. I couldn't say if he's still here in Memphis, but he was here for certain." She repeated her name and phone number.

"All right, Joe? Satisfied?"

Joe Blunt grunted as he walked off.

Styles threw him her middle finger toward his tail.

Joe Blunt turned on a heel, swung and snapped the back of his hand across her face. She stumbled, latched on to the woodwork but said nothing, didn't touch the red mark spreading on her cheek as he walked off.

Now they were out under the half moon and a sprinkling of Tennessee stars.

Wearing his beat-up work gloves and dragon jacket, Joe Blunt dumped the body in the trunk of Stillwell's car, a bedsheet serving as his shroud, his old toolbox rattling.

"Follow me," Joe Blunt said, failing to keep his voice down.

Lola Styles started along the alley toward her car.

"Take mine," Joe Blunt insisted, pointing to his old Ford pickup.

"Joe, you know I don't like to drive that thing."

"Nobody gives a damn what you like." He slammed the trunk.

She complied. She thought of herself as calloused over and beyond intimidation, excepting around Joe Blunt. Look how he handled that body. Like it was any old chore. Boone Stillwell was walking and talking and dreaming not 30 minutes ago.

She turned over the truck's engine, the thing tuned to roar, and recalled how Donnie Harry Bliss treated her kind and considerate. What a nice break. But now she was back to natural life. She was right where she belonged.

Joe Blunt stomped toward Stillwell's car, the dead kid's keys and little sap in his hand.

Oh yeah, it was bound to come to this, she thought as she watched Joe Blunt slide in. Eight years in Brushy for manslaughter didn't teach him a damned thing worth knowing. Sooner or later, he was going to kill somebody new. And sooner or later I was gonna be at his side when he did it.

The two-vehicle caravan started out for President's Island, and Lola Styles reviewed his plan: Bury the body where it would be found in a day or so. Nothing too fancy, seeing as this Donald Harry Bliss was a stranger to town. Something right close to the Wolf River or over by Round Lake, maybe a man letting his dog run free, a bow hunter out for deer. A body. Donald Harry Bliss killed him. Remember? He fought with the Stillwell boy. Somebody called it in.

Heading west, trailing up high, and now she reviewed her plan: Joe Blunt made her call the reward line. She had done Joe Blunt's bidding, more than aware he' d killed before, and she would tell the cops as much, if and when it came to that. Then Donnie Harry Bliss would be set free, the reward would come through to her, and she' d be gone to a place Joe Blunt would never know.

Meanwhile, driving Stillwell's rank car, the dead man's body cooling rapidly in the trunk, Joe Blunt knew his woman had fucked this Bliss character bareback, thinking she was some kind of hellcat daredevil, and surely they were seen together. And knowing Lola, wouldn't you just bet that his jism and her juices was on that sheet that now surrounded Stillwell's corpse?

Joe Blunt dug out his cell phone and punched the 888 number. His story would deviate slightly from the one his Lola told.

In her robe and slippers, Mrs. Brent took a call at home from one of the outside flacks Cerasus employed to work on Operation Bleak. Protocol had been that such off-hour interruptions were transmitted to Ian Goldsworthy rather than to Francis Cherry directly. But Ian Goldsworthy was no more, which suited Mrs. Brent. She found him disagreeable, a sycophant, crude.

She located Mr. Cherry at an upmarket bowling alley on 12th Avenue.

"Have her call me," Cherry said over the clatter of pins. "But wait ten minutes."

He pocketed the phone, spun on the soft leather stool and returned his attention to the lane. Out of the crowd had emerged a woman in a thigh-high leopard-print skirt who thought stupid was cute. She was giggling herself to a record-setting game: Eighth frame and in all earnestness she'd knocked down only two pins. You couldn't do that on a bet.

Her firm thighs and cheeky panties drew little porkpie hat–wearing men from throughout the place, but Cherry was fixed on history. The ninth frame began. She strode to the return and lifted a lime-green ball like it was an anvil; as she stood in place to strategize, she nibbled on her lip and ignored the hoots. Next she wriggled her hips, toddled to the line, swung her arm and released the ball, more or less placing it down and letting it roll. It proceeded slowly along the buffed wood, its aim surprisingly true. For a second, Cherry was demoralized. He was hoping for unprecedented ineptitude. But then the ball ran out of steam and veered to the gutter. "Ahhhh," went the crowd. She giggled and brought her manicured fingers to her lips. Men cheered as they surrounded her. A drink was brought forth. She beamed. Well, a satisfied Cherry thought as he stood, you go with what God gave you.

In gray pinstripe, he walked to 12th Avenue wearing the bowling shoes he'd swiped, leaving behind his Payless oxfords.

The phone buzzed. Cherry stared at the Hudson as he listened. *The Wall Street Journal*, he was told, had posted a story on its website identifying him as the source for the Times Square billboard and the drawing of Donald Harry Bliss.

"Who gave me up?" Cherry asked. He assumed he'd hear the name Ian Goldsworthy in the next second or so.

The flack replied, "I don't know, Mr. Cherry."

"What? I run a billboard in Times Square? Is that what I do? I put pictures up for tourists?"

The flack hesitated. She once had been a muckety-muck at American Express. Now she wasn't. "No, Mr. Cherry. You don't."

"And did you tell them that?"

"I told them I didn't know who was responsible."

"Meaning it could've been me."

"Mr. Cherry—"

"Get my ass out of the fire. Tell them their story is wrong and that you're looking into it." He was confident no one at the financial services firm who arranged for use of the billboard would squeal. They managed 340 million in Cherry dollars, all of which they' d invested in their own poorly performing products. "Then let it play out."

"They asked if you knew Donald Harry Bliss."

Unaware he was walking north, Cherry found himself facing an aircraft carrier moored on the Hudson. A pedestrian bridge invited him to cross, but he stayed on the east side of the avenue, a flurry of yellow taxis zooming by. "Who is Donald Harry Bliss?"

"The man on the billboard."

"Donald Harry Bliss. Nope. Don't know him."

"You know nothing about the case?"

"What case?"

"His wife. The hit."

"'The hit'?"

"The man who killed his wife was the son of the—"

"Ding. Time's up," Cherry said. He looked over his shoulder. His Rolls-Royce Ghost was trailing him at a pace that would shame a snail.

"Wait," the flack said quickly. "The reward. What should I tell them?"

"Dinner for two at Olive Garden," Cherry replied. Eighty-two thousand calls had come in, according to Koo Young-Soon. Cherry wanted them to stop. When Bliss contacted him, it wouldn't be for a reward.

Michael Koons made a U-turn on Hollywood Boulevard and parked in front of his favorite Mexican place, the one with the Jimi Hendrix star out front. They served pork tacos in lettuce cups. He ordered a shot of Cuervo Gold and a Dos Equis and asked the waiter to remove the tortilla chips, patting his stomach for emphasis. Koons weighed 111 pounds. It was closing in on midnight. The restaurant was all but empty.

Down the hatch went the tequila, and Koons held high the empty glass. Another arrived and he studied the liquor. Alcohol hit him hard; usually a second drink, especially on an empty stomach and a worried mind, sent him reeling. But, damn, what a day. Adios Jose number two.

Let's take it from the top: Isabel Jellico had worked an early-morning shift at the coffee shop. Then she went to the Higashi Honganji Buddhist Temple. "Find a TV, Isabel," he had told her. "Fox, CNN, something. Your father."

She cut the connection.

He sent her a text. You are about to be exposed.

No reply.

His next text: Dear Ms. Bliss.

Fuck, she replied.

The meeting in Sir Bernie's all-white conference room. The agency head sat at his customary spot at the glass table for 12, his seat elevated just so. Ten white high-back chairs were empty. In a wash of sunlight, Koons sat to Sir Bernie's left, facing the San Gabriel Mountains.

The Saudis…

Sir Bernie, who weighed 400 pounds if an ounce, wriggled his fingers into a side pocket of his white suit jacket. He placed three Hershey's Kisses on the table. He unwrapped one and popped it in his mouth.

"Refresh me," said Sir Bernie.

Film finance was already vague, Koons said. Insurance had yet to be secured. But if Judy goes negative pickup, it's somebody's bargain. We're not leveraged.

"Quite so," said Sir Bernie.

"But he can't extend his partners. Judy needs a bank."

After another chocolate, Sir Bernie rested his hands on his mountainous stomach. He squinted as he pondered.

Koons said, "The budget is at one hundred million. The Saudis were fronting forty-five." He assumed Sir Bernie recalled that film finance forecast the gross at $500 million.

"The British Film Council?" Koons suggested hopefully.

Another chocolate kiss disappeared.

Sir Bernie said, "Tell Mr. Judy we shall do our finest."

He rolled back his chair.

Koons stood.

Now, in the Mexican restaurant, he remembered Sir Bernie's parting words: "Opportunity beckons, young Michael."

After a long slow drink of cold beer, Koons withdrew his tablet to review notes. A list of private wealth management firms were in one column, hedge funds that backed slate financing in another, organizations like the German Federal Film Fund in a third, Gap and Supergap funders in yet another. Koons assumed Judy and his partners had already tapped most of these, which was why Judy wanted to leverage Sir Bernard on a second go-around.

The waiter arrived and, as he slid the plate of tacos on the table, stole a glance at Koons's notes.

"Lost your financing, huh?"

Koons nodded.

"If only you knew somebody with a whole lot of money, huh?"

"If only," Koons replied.

Saturday and Sunday came and went and where in God's name was Boone? After doing her damnedest to avoid his calls, she'd tried to get him four, five or maybe six times. No answer. Ginger was thinking he'd had the big idea to claim that reward for turning in Donald Harry Bliss, only to discover—probably when he was halfway to New York City with his stitches and all—what the reward was: a steaming pile of nothing. The story itself had dried up and died. As Cotillion said, "You can go back to calling him J.J. Walk, if you'd like."

But then Ginger Stillwell began to worry. Boone was out there all alone and that was not his thing. His mother left, his father died, his wife divorced him: Every time Boone got some love in his life, he'd ended up by himself and he wasn't too good like that. "I'm waiting at the port of lonely hearts," he once said, quoting Johnny Cash, spinning a bottle cap on the bar with an index finger. Ginger remembered she held out her hand. "Come on, Boone," she said as the jukebox offered something slow with a whistling pedal steel. "Let's see if you learned how to dance."

It being Monday, she'd done her wash downtown and brought the basket back to her bedroom. As a gentle wind fluttered her curtains, she dumped the clothes on the bed and started to separate and fold, towels over there in that pile, T-shirts in that one, her jeans stacked already before she drove home. She had a bunch of mismatched socks she wore under her boots. In passing, she recalled that when she was with that man the newspapers and Internet were calling Bliss, she took care to remove the socks as she took off her boots so he wouldn't think her foolish. Though foolish she had been.

Fresh glass of iced tea nearby, Ginger was over by the chest of drawers when she heard a knock on the door frame. Immediately, she knew it wasn't Boone. He would've barged right in, the screen door slapping behind him.

"Just a minute," she shouted, tucking the drawer shut.

There was the sheriff and with him stood old Vern Sevcik, who used to be Clarksdale police.

"Ginger," said Sevcik through the screen even before she reached the door. "We got some real, real bad news."

Fifty bucks to dye it Elvis black.

"We do it all the time, mister," said the woman with a silver '60s beehive as she dipped him toward the sink. She ran warm water on his sandy hair, traffic rolling by on a rainy day in the Ville. "I've got to tell you, though, it don't never look like much in the light of day."

He hadn't shaved since last week and had himself a good stubble. But his beard would grow in light brown with red flecks. He' d have to shave. A barber on Martin Luther King Drive took care of it, hot towel, lather, straight edge. He was the only white man in the shop and nobody gave a damn.

Prior to this morning, he hadn't been out of the dump on the north side since he arrived. He didn't know he was old news. He didn't know the newspapers let it die. Or that Francis Cherry's firm had been linked to the billboard.

No air-conditioning and 90 degrees more often than not. He read every book he' d bought at the bus station. He asked the guy who delivered Chinese to bring him a newspaper. He did—the local shopper. Big news was the flea market over on Lewis and Clark. An ad asked if he was right with Jesus. He saw Moira in their apartment building, her backpack filled with school supplies. He'd pressed the elevator button. He was going down, she was coming up. The smile on her face when the door opened and she saw him standing there. Suddenly, a naughty glint in her eye. "I can't," he'd said, trotting sideways, "I'm already late." He shouted, "Rain check?" as the doors eased together.

When the sun returned, he left the barbershop and walked over toward Fairground Park and bought a pair of reading glasses at a five-and-dime, Buddy Holly frames black and thick; they hid the teardrop scar near his right eye. Then he set out to find a place where he could get a new ID. Maybe a Missouri driver's license, maybe a faculty badge from Washington University or some place. Took him a while but he found where he needed to be. Conversation with a bartender always started the same way and he had it down to four moves. "You want to proof me? Good, because I lost my ID. Actually, I don't care if I find it. You sure your friend can fix me up?"

One hundred dollars for a cold beer and worth every cent.

By 9:30 p.m., he was Frank Niewidzialny of Miami, Missouri. Had his photo taken with the black hair and glasses. Got a Visa card too.

To test it out, the whole thing—hair, glasses, the ID—he went downtown, close to the local daily paper's home, figuring if he was still news, someone over there would know it. He was wearing new black jeans and a white oxford, the cuffs rolled to his biceps. Same brands as always.

He found a pub crowded with high-tech types in baggy polo shirts and sleeveless blouses, everybody in khakis, their hoodies and sweaters hung on the backs of the chairs. Music blared, the kind he imagined Pup enjoyed, all pumping rhythms and a synthetic swoosh. He looked at his prepaid cell. No calls. Koons said she was safe. He asked him to stop calling. Anything happens, Sam, er, Donnie, I'll let you know.

Don't let your thoughts wander, Bliss told himself. Be alert, at least a little while longer. Then withdraw.

He wriggled the phone back into his pocket. Soon the bartender arrived and looked right at him. Solid, hair cropped, maybe 35—a no-bullshit guy. Frank Niewidzialny pointed to the nearest tap. A tall frosty mug arrived, and Niewidzialny said he'd run a tab. The beer was so cold it stung his teeth.

He filled an empty space. Should've been the other way around, but it wasn't. A few months ago, yes. A couple years ago, yes. The day after Pup told him to go fuck himself, absolutely. Now a new life was building inside him, one he didn't deserve.

It didn't matter if he was in a pub on North Turner Boulevard, St. Louis, Missouri. If not him, someone else. He was nobody. Nine guys at a table across the room were sharing pitchers and fries. Any one of them could take his stool and it wouldn't change a thing. That couple in back, waiting on dessert. Didn't mean a damned thing to them if he was Donnie Bliss, Sam Jellico, Frank Niewidzialny or some toll taker on a ragged road to hell.

He looked at his phone again.

The music blasted four heavy beats to the bar. A waitress snuck behind the counter and gave the bartender a whirl. He tolerated it, but spun her back toward her station. Retreating, she looked right at Frank Niewidzialny. He nodded, then took a long pull on the beer, the mug covering his face. When he put it down, the waitress was back to work, her tray filled with mixed drinks.

He finished the beer. He gestured for another. Midnight had come and gone. People were pairing off all around. A good feeling in the place, laughter. Everybody at ease. A trivia game played on a TV monitor overhead: Denver Pyle, he answered silently.

The Samnite Wars. Eighteen. The Otis Elevator Company. I don't know.

He headed toward the men's room, navigating around tables and conversations.

Big room, as clean as could be expected. Several sinks, all with liquid soap. He looked at himself in the mirror. Dyed hair and bullshit glasses. Asshole.

If Moira ever saw him—

He turned.

There were newspaper pages in display cases above the urinals. He thought he saw…

He stepped aside to let a man pass.

The *Post-Dispatch*. Column left-hand side. National news.

BILLBOARD MAN WANTED FOR QUESTIONING

Dateline Memphis, TN.

A body. Boone Stillwell, 24, of Jerome, AZ.

Witnesses say…

Donald Harry Bliss, 40, formerly of New York City…

10

Ian Goldsworthy set up at the Cape Canaveral Motor Lodge below a rusted underpass on a grisly four-lane highway in Jersey City. He registered under the name Cecil Limpopo, a tribute to his adventures in Zimbabwe. An elderly woman who wore pink winged eyeglasses and a faded housecoat monitored the reception desk, a German shepherd at her side. Cash was preferred. At the hourly rate, a room would've billed out at $1,300 a day, but Goldsworthy negotiated a much, much lower charge. Then he explained his length of stay. Seeing the rusted, ready-to-tumble space-age-era sign outside with its twinkling stars and orbiting planets, he told the woman he was a writer working on a history of NASA's Project Mercury. "Good for you," she replied as she teetered off toward her blaring TV.

Muck bunched at the curb, broken glass and ancient plastic wrappers too. The asphalt lot was veined with cracks; weeds had pushed through. The CCTV camera above the office door, like the one behind the desk, was a dummy.

The noon sun high overhead, Ian Goldsworthy trudged toward his second-floor room, its door exposed and facing the highway, and was greeted by a strange, bestial scent when he opened the door. He'd experienced much worse: In a rundown

Port Louis, Mauritius, hotel, he woke from a heroin haze to find next to him in bed the torso of the teenage boy he'd been with several nights before. It had been at his side at least 12 hours. He'd forgotten all about it until this moment, and never found out who'd put it there.

Inside, a chair propped against the door, he took out a pint of Bombay gin and drank from the bottle. He was back in his element. Forty dollars got him a bit of rock from Debonair, a hazy transvestite who entertained truckers in the motel parking lot. "I'm here, sugar," he/she said when he asked about refills. A tug on Goldsworthy's genitals produced no additional business.

Of course, there was no Internet access at the Cape Canaveral, but a diner across the four-lane highway, a concrete slab for a divider, offered Wi-Fi. Goldsworthy ate three meals a day in a window booth while surfing far, wide and deep for information on Donald Harry Bliss. At night, as 18-wheelers and wailing police cars rocketed past his room, he slept in the chair, dreaming of the data he'd compiled, a smile on his face. He'd found several photos on the Web and a series of posts on Facebook that gave him a lead he intended to exploit.

Donnie Bliss had a daughter, Shara, who was a young teen in most of the photos. Under the name Isabel Jellico, Shara Bliss now was a student at the University of California at Los Angeles. She worked at the local Coffee Bean & Tea Leaf. She had written a novel. Hollywood was making it into a movie.

Cecil Limpopo began to plan his trip west.

On the evening of the fourth day of his stay at the Cape Canaveral, he looked out the diner window to see a navy Crown Victoria pass under the motel's sign on its way toward the front desk. Minutes later, the driver and her companion strolled up toward the yellow door to Goldsworthy's room. They entered with little difficulty. Goldsworthy couldn't tell if they were MI6 or

CIA. But he was impressed with their capabilities. He'd ditched the useless mobile Cherry had given him and hadn't bought a new one. No calls from his motel room either; one from the diner's pay phone. He used only cash. And yet they found him.

He wondered if they tracked him down through the only visitor he'd had—the man who gave him new papers, including a British passport, in exchange for $5,000 in cash, the money withdrawn from the belt Goldsworthy wore under his shirt morning, noon and night.

The agents who'd arrived in the Crown Vic lingered in his room. Goldsworthy made a second call from the pay phone. He was at Newark Airport 45 minutes later and on a flight to LAX 80 minutes after that.

Cecil Limpopo slept on the flight west and dreamed he was young again. He had his power. His mind and body hadn't yet corrupted by drugs, arrogance and a lack of accountability. He was beautiful. Boys sought him; rarely did he pay. Then the dream shifted and Cherry was standing over him, a chain saw in his hands.

Koo Young-Soon arrived by taxi and in a shopping bag carried a binder that ballooned with 612 11-by-17 pages of information culled from the 91,062 phone calls to the 888 number at Telephonic Data Exchange. He entered Madison Square Park, shrouded in midmorning clouds, and found Francis Cherry, who sat facing north, a statue of Chester A. Arthur nearby. Behind him, squeals of delight rose from the little chubby kids running in the playground, nannies on benches, their conversations in lilting English with Irish, Jamaican and Nigerian accents. Cherry eavesdropped but heard nothing useful. This morning, he floated a rumor that an army of badgers had escaped the hull of a cruise ship off the coast of Borneo and were feasting on passengers. A week or so ago, back when Donnie Bliss was still John Bleak, he'd put buy orders in on several cruise-lines companies. A quarter-point dip and the deals would kick in. A half-point recovery and the sell orders would go through. He stood to earn $800,000. Tip money.

"See right over there, Mr. Koo?" Cherry said when his taciturn investigator arrived. "No, there. There. Right. That's where Madison Square Garden used to be. Hence the name Madison Square Garden. What is that?"

Koo dropped the binder on the bench. It landed with a thud that vibrated Cherry's spine, not an unpleasant sensation.

"This is the data we collected from the phone calls," Koo said as he stood upright, feet spread, hands clasped behind his back. "Categorized and cross-referenced."

"Hoo-boy," Cherry said as he lifted the cover and thumb-flipped the endless pages. "Is there an executive summary?"

"In the forty months since Mr. Bliss was last seen in New York City, at the service for his late wife, Moira Riegel Bliss, we have reliable data to suggest he has spent at least several days in one hundred and two U.S. cities. He rented apartments in thirty-eight cities. Traveled by train seventy-nine times. Rented cars eleven times. He used the following aliases: John Bleak, Anthony Faithful, J.J. Walk, Lester Hope—"

"I see a pattern in those names."

"Yes, sir," Koo replied.

"Les Hope. That's as good as John Bleak."

"Yes, sir."

To Cherry, the young man seemed exhausted, though with his heavy eyelids and slack expression, who could tell?

"Continue."

"Thirty-six women say they dated him."

"'dated.' That's quaint."

"Fourteen. It seems more likely it was fourteen."

"Twenty-two women lied about sleeping with a man wanted for questioning in a murder investigation just to claim the reward. Is that what our culture is coming to, Mr. Koo?"

Chin high, Koo cleared his throat. "We have four hours and eleven minutes of video that place Mr. Bliss in various cities."

"The bogus crap that's on YouTube?"

"This is from airport security, Amtrak security, from ATM machines, hotels. Drugstores, supermarkets. Intersections."

"I'm guessing you developed some kind of grid."

"Pages nine and ten."

"It says…"

"He likes cities that have a light-rail system."

"And?"

"He prefers the south in winter."

"Well, he's no idiot."

"And he's been to Los Angeles more often than any other city. Quite often three years ago. Less so in time. Except for—"

"I know. Bodies in the street, blood. How do these things happen?"

Cherry stood. Koo bent to lift the binder.

When Koo was upright again, Cherry rested his hand on his back and steered him until he turned south. Already, a queue was forming at the fancy-schmancy burger shack over there. Cherry checked his watch. In three minutes, a man would exit the shack and hand him two Chicago-style hot dogs. Cherry decided he would give one to Koo Young-Soon.

They walked along a path, elm trees thick on either side, brawny insurance company skyscrapers towering above.

"I realize you're a numbers guy, Mr. Koo," Cherry said, "but did you find anything that's not quantifiable? I mean, I know it's blasphemy, but—and I say this with all due regard and appreciation—did you come up with anything I can use?"

His eyes fixed on what's ahead, Koo said, "He has a daughter."

"I read that in the *Post*."

"She's a screenwriter."

"The *Post*."

"The movie she wrote is in financial trouble. It's worse than has been reported."

Cherry skidded to a halt.

"Yes," said Koo in quiet triumph.

"How do you know this?"

"Her agent called the hotline." Koo chose not to mention the man had been drinking.

"Who is he?"

"Michael Koons." He added the name of the agency.

Out came Cherry's cell phone. Seconds later, Mrs. Brent answered. Yes, a Michael Koons had also called the office. Several times.

"You want to go to Hollywood?" Cherry said, looking up.

"Who doesn't want to go to Hollywood, Mr. Cherry?"

Up ahead, a man waited with two hot dogs.

"There is another item," Koo said as they strolled the sun-dappled path. "Whether Bliss had something to do with the killing of a man in Memphis...He was in St. Louis at the time."

"You have tape?"

Koo nodded.

"Hold on to it," Cherry said. "Its value can only increase."

"Oh sweet Jesus," Ginger said, a frilled handkerchief in her hand. "Didn't he look like he was just asleep on that slab?"

Cotillion nodded. The autumn sun hung low over Memphis, casting shadows. The women from out west were on a long, wide avenue near the Shelby County Medical Examiner's office, which was situated in an old redbrick Eye, Ear, Nose and Throat hospital. Ginger had signed the papers, and now the body was going to be shipped to the funeral parlor in Cottonwood.

They needed to get back too. Johnny Eagle said he'd put up the money for Ginger to fly to Memphis, but she preferred Cotillion's company, knowing full well she couldn't do it alone—identify the body, stand for questioning by the police, look over official papers. "I need you both here," said Johnny Eagle without sentiment as he turned over his car keys. "Be quick about it."

Took them 22 hours to drive across Arizona, New Mexico, the Texas Panhandle, Oklahoma and Arkansas into Tennessee, Johnny Eagle's station wagon good on I-40, steady like it could take it all by itself. Cotillion did most of the driving, Ginger most of the talking. She insisted it was her fault Boone had gone east so therefore it was her fault he was dead.

They pulled in at 11:30 at night. As a courtesy, Memphis PD made sure they got a good rate at the Econo Lodge.

This morning, a detective said, "Ma'am, we just don't know who did it."

"I just don't know either," Ginger replied through her tears. Boone's personal effects in a small manila envelope rested on her skirt.

The detective went back to flattening down his necktie and sneaking a look at his watch. He had black hair, perfectly combed, and a Van Dyke, meticulously trimmed.

"Did anybody call up to tell you where Boone was since he left the hospital?" Cotillion asked.

"I'm not at liberty to say, ma'am."

"You put his picture in the newspaper."

Detective Sipp nodded.

Cotillion continued. "I read on the Internet your murder rate is down by twenty-five percent."

“That’s right.”

“So you’ve got the time…”

Ginger looked up.

“Ma’am.” Sipp sighed. “I assure you and your friend here we will do our best.”

Now, outside the medical examiner’s, Cotillion said, “We’d better go pick up Boone’s car and get out on the road. We ought to get in a few hours before sunset.”

Ginger managed a nod. They’d already agreed that she would drive Johnny Eagle’s wagon and Cotillion would follow in Boone’s car. They’d go as far as they could until exhaustion set in. The 1,400-mile route was dotted with motels and rest stops.

The car was in the impound lot, which wasn’t too far from the highway. Papers needed to be signed, the vehicle examined. When the attendant popped the trunk, Ginger frowned. They cleaned it up, the front and back seats too. She imagined technicians had been looking for blood and such, and in doing so removed all trace of Boone.

Nevertheless, to her mind the car was a coffin with wheels.

“You want to check the contents?” the attendant asked.

“Such as?” she asked wearily.

“There’s some medicine in the glove box. Pepto. Some CDs. A shot glass.”

Out of the corner of her eye, Ginger noticed Boone’s toolbox had been cleaned as well. Probably after they searched for fingerprints, she thought, like on TV.

“It’s all on that sheet,” he added as he handed over the clipboard and pen. The setting sun was in his eyes.

With Cotillion peering over her shoulder, Ginger looked over the short list, which included the contents of the glove compartment, the trunk and the toolbox. One beer can, worth five cents on return, had been found under the seat.

Ginger clicked the pen top and readied to sign her name.

Then she said, "Hey. Hold on. Where's Ol' Buddy?" She turned to Cotillion. "His gun. Ol' Buddy. It's not on the list."

"Maybe—"

"Maybe nothing," Ginger said. "Boone would've sold his wedding ring before giving up Ol' Buddy."

Joe Blunt drove his truck deep into President's Island. The private homes and street lights disappeared, and now they were moving toward wilderness, bouncing on ruddy roads, his high beams sweeping across an army of trees. They were away from where they' d buried the body, but the natural environment was much the same.

"It's time for you to come forth," he said as he threw the truck into park. They were on a bare patch deep in the forest. When he cut the lights, the night's darkness swallowed them whole.

Exasperated, Lola Styles said, "Joe, we already—"

"It's time for you to come forth."

"Joe, what are you talking about?" She turned to face him. "It's already fucked."

"It ain't so fucked it can't be repaired," he replied. Dragon jacket unzipped, he was in one of his black sleeveless muscle shirts despite the chill.

"How? I mean, what's there to gain? The reward is worthless."

"I see it as there's a new kind of reward."

Lola Styles said, "Huh?"

Joe Blunt said, "The goddamn newspapers said Bliss was rich."

"They said his in-laws was rich, Joe. They didn't say nothing about him."

Joe Blunt shook his head. "He's got money."

"Joe, if he's got money, he sure wasn't showing it. I saw him, remember?"

"You fucked him. Remember?"

"Ah, for shit's sakes, Joe. Let it go. You think I care about every bimbo you fuck wherever it is you run off to?"

"Get him back here."

"Joe, if I could, don't you think I would?"

With that, Joe Blunt reached over and smacked her on the forehead.

She grabbed him by the wrist and held tight. "Enough of that, Joe."

With little effort, Joe Blunt snapped free.

He said, "You're going to the cops and you're telling them Bliss stole a sheet from your bed."

Annoyed, she said, "And why the fuck would he do that, Joe? Steal my sheet."

He flexed his fist, showing his star tattoo. "Man ain't killed before. He's not thinking clear."

She couldn't fathom where to begin to count the flaws embedded in his logic. "You want me to tell the cops Bliss killed Boone in my apartment?"

"Don't be stupid, Lo. Repeat what you said: They was fighting after you two got together, and you came home and the sheet was gone."

"Oh Jesus, Joe…"

"You insist and they got to bring him back," Joe Blunt said. "Step up. Call the newspapers, the TV. Let them put a local face to the claim. You go in and you swear up and down that Bliss killed that little bastard and they got to bring him back."

"No they don't." She folded her arms under her heavy breasts. The Sun Studio logo rose as she huffed. "He's gone, Joe. It's done. Face the fact."

"They bring him back and I'll deal with him."

"You're going to blackmail Billboard Man?"

Joe Blunt stared into the darkness. "Do it, Lo," he said. He thumbed a button and his headlights produced ghost shadows in the mist.

Sipp was no more thrilled to see them at night than he had been during the day. The lead detective tried to hide his amusement whenever Ginger said Ol' Buddy, a phrase that was near breaking Cotillion's heart.

"I'm saying that Boone had Ol' Buddy with him up until the moment somebody killed him. After, probably, too."

"I understand that, ma'am."

"So wouldn't you think whoever killed him has it?"

"Not necessarily, ma'am." Sipp looked over at Cotillion, waiting for her to snap at him.

Ginger said, "You're saying you think the killer pawned it."

"Or tossed it in the Mississippi," he said. "But no, ma'am, listen, please." He leaned in and folded his hands on his desk. "I understand what you're trying to do and we appreciate your help and all, but—"

"Come on, Ginger," Cotillion said as she stood. She held out her hand. "We're not wanted."

"Now hold on there."

"Ginger."

"Ma'am—"

Out they went past the coffee room to the elevator, and if the detective chased after them, they didn't hear him coming.

Then they were on Poplar Avenue, crossing the huge parking lot, and now they were going to have to go back to the pound to get Boone's car. Cotillion knew they'd be lucky to pass Little Rock by midnight. And Ginger was crying again.

Whatever warmth the late October sun gave the day was long gone. Cotillion heard herself say, "Oh, Ginger, I know it's so unfair..."

Ginger stopped to dig through her bag for her handkerchief. "It's the final indignation, isn't it? The one thing his father gave him and somebody took it."

"You couldn't do more than ask," Cotillion replied. She inched away, encouraging her friend to keep moving. She wouldn't be so cruel as to remind her that she'd left her kids with her 84-year-old grandmother, but it might come to that.

"Did I mention Ol' Buddy had a white handle?" Ginger said as she caught up. "He used to say it was pearl. But I don't know."

Out of the corner of her eye, Cotillion saw a man crossing the parking lot. He seemed to be walking directly toward them. But people had business with the Memphis police from dawn to dawn.

"To be honest with you, I don't even know if Boone had any bullets for Ol' Buddy. Wouldn't it be just like him to—"

Cotillion turned at the sudden silence.

Ginger stared at the man as he approached.

Black hair, thick glasses, stubble. Tall, in his 40s. A blue blazer, white oxford shirt, black jeans, sneakers.

"I didn't do it," the man said as he opened his palms and held them wide at his sides.

Ginger said, "J.J.?"

Cotillion stepped between them.

"Hand to God," Donnie Bliss replied. He stopped. "I had nothing to do with it."

"Not nothing," Cotillion told him.

11

Donnie Bliss had barbecue sent over to the Econo Lodge. It was the least he could do.

Ginger and Cotillion each sat on a double bed, and he sat on the floor in the space behind the desk and the chest of drawers. "I came to talk to the cops," he told them. "From St. Louis." He said he flew under his own name.

"And that would be Donald Harry Bliss," Ginger said with a trace of bitterness.

Yes. Though no one had called him that since the day it was typed on his birth certificate.

He was certain he'd been seen on the train leaving Tennessee. A young waitress talked to him in Carbondale. The woman who dyed his hair in St. Louis could attest to where he'd been. As could the man who took a straight razor to his beard.

"Everywhere you go, you're just passing through," Ginger said, legs tucked beneath her. Out of her dress and back in jeans and a long-sleeved T, her soft, musty boots on the carpet. She'd draped a bath towel on the bed; pork rib bones rested on a Styrofoam plate alongside a plastic fork and knife. Ginger had some of the dry rub on her cheeks. "No roots."

No roots, no.

Cotillion said, "Your wife, though…"

Bliss looked down at his empty plate. It was part of the conversation again.

He said, "A man killed her. Instead of killing me."

"I'm sorry," Ginger said.

They ate in silence for a little while.

Cotillion had kicked off her shoes. One long leg hung off the side of the bed. "The question is, if you didn't kill Boone, who did?"

That's the question, yes.

"Me, I don't believe much in coincidence," Ginger added as she bit open the little hand-wipe package.

"It could've been just about anybody," Cotillion said as she stood. "Boone could've been in a mood and it blew up on him."

Bliss stood too. He brought his plate to the trash can.

"What do you think happened?" Ginger asked.

He said, "They told you they found him wrapped in a sheet."

"He was in somebody's house," Cotillion said, picking up the thread.

"He met somebody. Boone," Ginger said.

They turned to stare at her. Cotillion said it: "He was out here trying to win you back. He's not about to fall into somebody's bed."

"So why was he in somebody's house?"

Bliss said, "Maybe he told someone he knew I' d been here."

"For the damned reward," Ginger spit. "Oh, Boone. He kept calling me and calling me…"

"But did he say where he was?" Cotillion asked as she crossed toward the bathroom.

Ginger said no. She looked at Bliss. "Who saw you here?"

The question caught him by surprise. "I was gone by the time it mattered," he replied.

"Not what I asked."

He said, "I don't know."

The bathroom light went on and Cotillion spoke over running water. "Could you make a list?"

A list. He rode the trolleys. He walked the night. He slept under a tree in Audubon Park and woke to find a small dog licking his face.

"I could double back," he said.

Cotillion cut the water flow. She emerged with a towel in her hands. "You'd do that?"

Bliss nodded. He had no idea how he could disappear again.

Ginger left the bed, a sense of pride shining through grief: J.J. was a good man after all. "Well then, I'm in," she said as she scooped up her trash.

Cotillion said, "I know you two have a terrible thing in common and, Ginger, I know you have it in your mind to set things right. But it's time to go home."

Bliss ran a thumb along the corner of his lip. "I'm going to see the police. I can—"

"No," Ginger said, "I got to see it through."

She had $46 in her purse, not half enough to pay for another night at the Econo Lodge.

"If you don't mind driving back Johnny Eagle's wagon…"

"No, that's fine by me," Cotillion said. "But the funeral, Ginger."

"Flight could have both of you back in Phoenix by midmorning," Bliss said. He had $1,400 in his sneaker, buried along with the papers that said he was Frank Niewidzialny.

"No, I'm staying," Ginger said.

What the hell. He had a Rolls-Royce at home so he might as well have one in Hollywood too.

So thought Francis Cherry, who now wore on his lap a portable video monitor with all sorts of scientific gizmos and doo-dads. They'd allow him to eavesdrop on the conversation Koo Young-Soon was about to have and witness it as well, even though he was sitting in his Rolls over by a towering temple on Santa Monica Boulevard and Koo was in that big building over there in Century City.

Problem, though: Koo was taller than everybody he met, including the security guards, so all Cherry had seen thus far was a parade of foreheads. "Sit, Koo," said Cherry into the invisible earpiece the young giant wore.

Koo, who was in an elevator on his way up, was confused for a moment. But he was clever enough to understand what Cherry meant. On the cross-country flight in Cherry's private jet, he had gained some insight into this Mr. Francis Cherry, a mastermind for mischief with unfettered faith in man's fallibility. Cherry told him as much when the chateaubriand was served medium well.

"Sooner or later, everybody fucks up," he said as he threw down a dollop of Dijon mustard. "What do you say, Koo? We tell the chef we're tossing him out over Colorado?"

Now the receptionist stood as Koo passed between the sliding glass doors. Blonde and perfectly proportioned with flawless teeth, she radiated. As Koo drew nearer to her desk, the micro-camera panned upward and she disappeared. Cherry was looking at the agency's logo.

"Back up," he said.

The driver, thinking Cherry was addressing him, shifted the car in reverse.

Koo did as instructed and once again Cherry was looking at physical perfection.

"Michael Koons," said Koo. The speck of a camera was below the knot of his polka-dotted tie.

"You are Mr. Koo," the receptionist said. "Michael is eager to see you."

"I'll bet he is," said Cherry as the Rolls retreated along sunny Selby Avenue.

About a crow-flying mile away was Ian Goldsworthy, who once again left the Coffee Bean & Tea Leaf in Westwood with no more than he had going in. The social-networking sites provided much of what he needed on Shara Bliss, aka Isabel Jellico, and a whole lot of gossip too—everything but where she was now.

He'd visited her apartment, knocking on neighbors' doors and waiting for the postman in case she'd moved on and her mail needed forwarding. He'd been across the village green of the UCLA campus, lingering to no avail at the Student Activities Center and fast-food shops. All these fresh faces had no idea where she'd gone. He began to envy her for the loyalty of her mates, who were hiding her.

He discovered the production company Blabberdashery was a shell: no offices, no personnel. But he had her agent's name and addresses, office and home.

A new strategy, then. Off to Staples for business cards. Now he was Cecil Limpopo, a producer for 5★. A new TV reality show: *Shall We Marry a Duke?* "Well, you'd be a duchess then, wouldn't you?" he told one young girl in Westwood Village. He met a young man in the producers program at UCLA in a line snaking out the door of a cookie shop. He was looking to land soft. An AP job at *Marry a Duke*? Why not?

"She's got a grandfather," the young man said. "Up in Mendocino County."

That would be Harry Bliss, thought Goldsworthy.

"Well done, son."

The agent. The grandfather. Which? To what end?

Though tidy with a lavender plant on his credenza, Michael Koons's office wasn't suitable for a meeting with a representative of Francis Cherry. So he commandeered Sir Bernie's white conference room. After trying out Sir Bernie's perch, he regathered the financials and hurried to the tail end of the long glass table. Then he went to welcome Koo Young-Soon, who, as Blake in reception had reported, was an unyielding giant. His hand swallowed Koons's.

The agent was dressed in blue pinstripe with a mauve shirt and, showing respect to his Wall Street visitor, a necktie. Usually, Koons traveled the agency without shoes, but for this meeting he'd slipped into his black A. Testoni alligator loafers over his mauve socks.

Droopy-eyed Koo wore a gray suit off the rack.

Koons led him toward a seat with his back to the sky above the San Gabriel Mountains.

"Sit in his chair," Cherry instructed from the Rolls outside the temple.

Koo did as he was told.

Recovering quickly, Koons said, "Something to drink?" He moved the financials toward his guest.

"Fresca and cactus juice on the rocks," Cherry said.

"No thank you," Koo said.

"Then should we jump right in?" Koons asked as he sat.

Koo nodded once.

"Well then…" Koons said with a sigh. Butterflies fluttered in his stomach, his old-school Librium having no effect. There was too much riding on this deal.

"Put your hand on the book," Cherry said. "Leave it there. Stare at him."

"If you look at the numbers, Mr. Koo, you'll see it's as I indicated. Everything is in place. If you were to ask, the Saudis would tell you the risk is minimal."

"Don't blink, Koo," said Cherry, who was eating an orange Popsicle as he stared at the monitor.

Koo felt an urge to open the bound book. Faced with columns of numbers, he would be on solid footing. Without, the situation in the white room was even more surreal. He would find no bearing. Add to his state of mind the fog of jet lag and Koo already felt as if he were in a cloud. With Cherry a little red devil on his shoulder.

Koons's eyes shifted from Koo's eyes to his hand on the book. From his hand to his eyes. He began to go moist under his collar.

"Where would you like to begin, Mr. Koo?"

"Say 'As you wish,'" Cherry told him.

"As you wish."

"Mr. Koo," Koons said, "I gather you've already examined the numbers. Would you mind if I ask where you got them?"

"No," said Koo.

"No, as in you wouldn't mind?"

Cherry said, "Take a shot, Koo."

"I'm not prepared to say," Koo replied.

"I see," Koons said.

"Not bad, Koo. For the next sixty seconds, you're on your own."

Liberated, Koo opened the book and tilted it just so.

Cherry read along with him. All film budgets were bullshit, but a source of amusement too. Up at 3 a.m., he'd begun the day by going over Isabel Jellico's script: pretty good; goddamn if he didn't want to know who done it. Immediately, though, he knew the director would want to re-create mid-19th century Manhattan on a back lot, and the unions would pad the living shit out of construction costs. Cherry made a call. The sets for *Gangs of New York* were still up at Cinecitta Studios in Rome. There's $10 million off the top line right there, and besides, the Mayor's Office of Film in New York would waive all sorts of fees for him so they could shoot on location on the Lower East Side and in Chinatown. Also, Cherry knew the producers saw franchise in the story, so they were front-loading many of the long-term costs into the first budget and would dole out net points on less expensive sequels to keep the team on board. Cherry figured he could balance the costs and cleave out another bunch of millions from the first film.

Then he phoned Riyadh.

A grandnephew of the Prince Sultan took the call.

"Mr. Cherry," he said with practiced composure. "It has been too long."

"Cannes, right? You were the man, Fahd."

"It was entertaining."

"At least," Cherry said. "Listen, I'm trying to find out why your film commission is bailing on this picture." He read the title.

"Now you are taking over Hollywood, Mr. Cherry?"

"If you say it's a dog, it's a dog."

The return call came within the hour. In his suite, Cherry was lounging in a Jacuzzi so long and deep it could've used a diving board. He listened.

"Fahd, you are still the man. *Shukran Jazilan.*"

Now, when the 59th second had passed, Cherry said, "Koo. Close the book. Close your eyes. Count to four."

Koo did as told. The budget numbers scurried in the darkness. They made no sense. Conceding naïveté, Koo reminded himself to ask Cherry why a film, if excellent, would require promotional resources three times the cost of production.

"Stand, Koo."

"Mr. Koo…" Koons said as he scrambled out of his chair. "Is there anything—"

"Everything appears to be in order," Koo said without prompting. They'd rehearsed this part on the short ride over from Beverly Hills.

Koons buttoned his jacket. "Can I ask which way you're leaning, Mr. Koo?"

"I am authorized to take a decision on Mr. Cherry's behalf."

"Damn it, Koo. String him along," Cherry said.

Koons said, "I don't mean to be impertinent, but Blabberdashery—"

"Blabberdashery," said Cherry to himself. "I love that."

"—is up against certain deadlines."

"Mr. Cherry is ready to proceed."

Koons gripped the back of the white-leather chair for balance. "He'll front the entire fifty million dollars?" Quickly, he added, "Excuse me for being so blunt."

Forty-six million, Koo thought. "Yes."

"Oh that's—"

"On one condition."

Popsicle stick in his cheek, Cherry inched up on the backseat and stared at the monitor. Oooh, let it drip off your tongue, Koo…

"Mr. Cherry insists that Shara Bliss be in his office at eight o'clock on Monday morning."

Koons stumbled. "I'm sorry."

"This is nonnegotiable. Monday. Eight o'clock."

"Mr. Koo, I don't know that I can—"

Koo thrust his giant hand toward the agent. "Thank you for your time."

Alongside the temple, a deeply satisfied Francis Cherry clapped his hands once and rubbed them together with vigor. Hoo-boy, that was fun. He expected a more amusing reaction and some stuttering pushback, but what the hell. Stunned silence worked too.

Removing the earpiece and microphone, he flicked the driver's earlobe. "Go pick up the kid," he said, pointing south. "I don't want him walking in traffic."

Maybe it was the toot before leaving the Pacific Palisades, or the Bombay gin he had for breakfast, but Goldsworthy floated on the lilt of optimism as he drove toward Century City, the bright sun a testament to the miracle that was Southern California, where the weather ensured nothing could go wrong, not ever. He looked into the rearview mirror and saw not the sagging under his rheumy eyes, the sallow tint to his skin, the lines crisscrossing his forehead, the tiniest fray in his collar. He saw a man on the go!

Maybe he'd been wrong all these many years in avoiding responsibility and leadership. From the moment he arrived at the Cape Canaveral in Jersey City to the acquisition of new papers for travel, from the interviews in and around UCLA to the formation of the bogus production company 5★, he had demonstrated exceptional foresight. Everything came together in the best way possible. He had options. He could zig or zag.

And lo and behold, there on Santa Monica Boulevard was a parking space. And with time on the meter yet. The gods were on his side. Welcome back, he told them, as he stepped into sunlight and slipped into his suit coat. We're on our way toward another great advent—

On the other side of the boulevard: Francis Cherry.

Francis Cherry with a Rolls-Royce. And an Asian giant.

Cherry patted the giant on the arm. He reached up and tapped him tenderly on the cheek.

As the driver opened the back door, Cherry stepped aside and let the giant precede him. The giant sat, impassive but content.

Retreating, Goldsworthy groped for the parking meter.

His stomach rumbled. Acid rushed into his throat.

Cherry. Here.

He had been outwitted again.

And in all the time Goldsworthy had worked for him, never once had Cherry expressed his gratitude with such open joy.

A pat on the arm. A tap on the cheek.

The rental-car keys dropped from Goldsworthy's hand.

When he bent to retrieve them, he lost his balance and stumbled onto the boulevard.

When he gained his equilibrium, he saw that Cherry, his giant and the Rolls-Royce were gone.

He opened the passenger's side door and sat with his feet on the pavement.

He needed someone to tell him what to do.

His phone rang.

"Hello," said a young, nervous voice. "I'm interested in appearing on *Marry a Duke*. How do—"

Goldsworthy dropped the mobile to the sidewalk and crushed it with his heel.

12

They decided to go to the police station in the morning. Donnie Bliss left the Econo Lodge. He took a room near a minor-league baseball stadium, not too far from the hotel and on the same long thoroughfare as Sun Studio. He registered under his own name.

He stared at the stadium, a used paperback book on his lap.

For a while, he put his feet up on the window ledge. He began to doze off.

"Donald," Moira said. They were walking along First Avenue. A sunny New York Sunday. Where was everybody?

"Donnie," he replied.

"I don't know...Donnie. It's a boy's name. You're not a boy."

Arm in arm. She saw the possibilities. Until then, he didn't realize that you knew when it was right. He'd never loved a woman before.

He had a girlfriend back when he should've been in high school, and he loved her with his teenager heart. But that was another story.

"Did you ever use Harry?" Moira wore her black hair short then, but it was long now in his dream.

He looked at her in disbelief.

"I withdraw the question," said the lawyer's daughter. She laughed. "Let's try: Did you ever think of changing your name?"

No.

"If you did."

I wouldn't.

"If you did, what would it be?"

He thought for a moment.

He said, "Donnie Riegel."

Her family name.

She stopped. "Donnie?"

They kissed right there on First Avenue.

Detective Sipp listened. What choice did he have? That Indian over there was weighing his reaction to every word.

Bliss sat between the two women, Sipp on the other side of the table. Three paper cups of coffee. The detective brought in his own mug. Bliss was dressed in his blazer over a white oxford. His hair was still ink black. He had a faint scar across his lip and a teardrop scar near his right eye.

Her long black hair tied in back, Cotillion wore a yellow peasant blouse over a gold T. Ginger Stillwell had on a gray shirt with butterfly buttons. All three wore jeans.

"Let me see if I've got this." Sipp tugged on his tidy Van Dyke. "You were in St. Louis when…when Mrs. Stillwell's husband was killed."

Bliss had already mentioned the witnesses. He told him about the bus ride from Carbondale. He said more people would've seen him if he hadn't worked so damned hard to be invisible.

Sipp didn't know whether to tell Bliss and the women about the anonymous tip they' d received on the hotline: In plain sight, Billboard Man was arguing with the late Boone Stillwell. It looked like it could've turned violent. Probably did. Probably got out of hand real quick.

"Did you see Mr. Stillwell while you were here?" Sipp asked.

No.

"Did you know he was here?"

"How could he know that?" Ginger said. She'd been sitting quietly, knowing Cotillion would speak up if anything went awry.

"I don't know, Mrs. Stillwell. Maybe you told him. That is a possibility, isn't it?"

"She didn't," Donnie Bliss said.

Nodding toward Bliss, Cotillion said, "We didn't know he was here. Not before and not until last night."

Sipp reached for his coffee. "All the same, here we are…"

Eager to leave, Cotillion stole a glance at the time on her cell phone.

"I have a question for you," Ginger said, elbows on the table. "How did you know Mr. Bliss was here?"

"Other than he just said so?" the cop asked.

Cotillion said, "Her question seems reasonable to me."

Bliss knew the answer. The promise of a reward meant all sorts of information had been flowing freely. Somebody tipped off Memphis PD.

"Somebody told you they saw me with her husband," he said, nodding toward Ginger.

Sipp conceded that was so.

"That was a lie," Cotillion said before Bliss could speak.

"You're going to have to figure out who would do that. Who would lie," Ginger said. "That's the person who killed Boone."

"Just like that, huh?" Sipp went.

Bliss thought that was about right. "I talked to one person while I was here," he said.

"The entire time you were in Memphis, you talked to one person?" the cop asked.

"I think he's saying—" Ginger said.

"A conversation of substance." The cop nodded.

"Lola Styles," Bliss said. "She lives over by the river, near the Biloxi Box plant. Works at Sun Studio."

"That ought to be easy enough for you to find," Cotillion said.

They expected he'd leave after they'd spoken to the police, but Bliss told the women he was staying. He could've crafted a story about wanting to find out how he fit into Stillwell's murder. He could've said something about it being the right thing to do. Or how he was upset that his name appeared in the newspapers, on local news and on the Web in association with a crime. But he didn't. He had nowhere else to go. He'd checked his phone. Nobody called.

Ginger said she was staying too.

"There's nothing here for you," Cotillion told her.

They were in the corridor, not far from the room where Sipp interviewed them. The water cooler buzzed. The linoleum begged for a mop.

"Nevertheless..." Ginger said. She took a handkerchief from her purse. Then, as tears began to fall, she retreated to the restroom.

Cotillion said, "You slept with this Lola Styles, didn't you? And you didn't tell Sipp."

"He'll know soon enough."

"Was that for Ginger's sake? So you can pick it up again?"

No, I'm not going to do that.

"What's wrong with you? Don't you see how fragile she is? Didn't you see it back in Jerome?"

"No," he said. "I didn't. I had no idea."

"So what is it about us that draws you in? I mean it. If it's not us, if it's not who we are, what is it?"

He shrugged.

"The same thing. Why not say it? The same damned thing."

He said, "There's something more."

"Something more. Then my question is, why? What is it you need from us?"

He knew the answer. But he didn't reply.

"So then what about someone like me? Does it matter that I'm a mom, that I've got plans? You'd just throw me down and then toss me aside too? One and done?"

"You should take her with you," he said.

"And then what? Her husband was killed trying to track you down, the man who made him out a fool in his hometown, and she's supposed to go back like nothing happened."

"Something happened."

"You happened. Maybe you'll think about that next time. Maybe you'll remember there's a person there too."

He was going to tell her she had him wrong. That he meant no harm. It was just a thing, a good time for two. But he recalled how Ginger wanted him to stay. He hadn't seen the need in her, no, but now he remembered it had been there all along.

He said, "She may not be safe in that hotel."

"She won't leave."

"Tell her I'll let her know what happens."

Cotillion said, "Well, she might believe that. But I don't."

Later, as he settled Ginger Stillwell in his hotel, he said, "Can I ask you a question?"

Ginger was stuffing her clothes into a pillowcase. There was a laundry room on the first floor. "Go ahead."

With his dyed-black hair and stubble, he was standing way over there, leaning on the door to keep it open.

"Why is your friend so peevish?"

"Peevish?" She smiled. "I never heard it called that before. I always say Cotillion doesn't suffer fools gladly."

He watched as she looked down at what she was wearing.

She knew the long-sleeved top needed a wash and so did the jeans, the only pair she brought along. If she was going to stay until the police told her something she could believe, she needed to clean them too.

He pointed to the dress she'd folded and put on the bed.

"I don't think I'd be comfortable if you stayed..."

He told her his room number.

She said, "Cotillion's a friend. Good and wise."

He nodded as he stepped into the hall and let the door close.

Michael Koons returned early to his Santa Monica condo and, much to his relief, there she was on the sofa, spread out, elbow dug into a cushion, head on her palm, an old black-and-white film on TCM. Textbooks and paperbacks, a yellow legal pad and a can of orange soda surrounded her laptop.

She wore denim bib overalls and a sleeveless T-shirt. Not long ago, she'd cropped her hair to little more than stubble. Koons didn't dare say it, but she'd inherited her father's good looks and then some; even in a town brimming with beauty, she was striking, more so because she didn't want to be.

"Hi," she said without turning to him.

Koons dropped his keys on the kitchen island, which was made of granite dyed mauve and ash. High on the 22nd floor, from where he stood Koons could see past the balcony's sliding doors to the endless sky and the blue Pacific.

He brought his loafers to his bedroom, hung his jacket on the valet stand. When he returned, his mauve socks disappeared into eggplant shag.

He sank into the plum armchair.

"What do I call you?"

She spun to sit. "I've been thinking about that. You know, being bored witless here in Santa Monica. Under house arrest. Michael."

"Hold that thought," Koons said. He went to retrieve a bottle of sparkling water flown in from Italy. Sir Bernie once said Fellini's agent drank it by the barrel. Returning, he said, "I think you stay with Isabel Jellico. Your nom de plume."

"My mother loved Shara," she replied wistfully. "I sort of do too."

"That little girl in your story? The one he's trying to rescue? Change her name to Shara."

"Oh, I don't know about that…" She sipped her soda, leaving an orange mustache.

"Let's go with Isabel. At least for this conversation. Because I have news."

She stretched out again, now tucking her bare feet under her legs.

"It looks like we've secured the financing."

"That's good."

Koons didn't believe she was so blasé. Her father once said she was all subtext. You have to watch as much as listen, Michael. Unless she's adamant, she won't tell you what she feels.

"A big pile of money," Koons said. "A *big* pile of money."

"The Saudis?"

"Homegrown."

"Some cool rockin' daddy. Sweet."

Koons smiled.

"You did this?" she asked.

"I did. Yes."

"What's the catch?"

"No catch." Koons took a long slow drink. "Well, there's one. Minor, though."

Isabel raised an eyebrow.

"You have to go to New York."

She sprang to her feet. "No."

"Isabel..."

"Absolutely not." She began to pace.

Koons stood and stepped in front of her. When she spun away, he trotted to face her again. "Oh, don't be so predictable, Isabel. Don't be so eighteen."

She stopped. Towering over him, she said, "Don't joke about it."

"Never. But—"

"I won't go."

"We fly on Sunday to Newark, stay in Soho, take the meeting, back to Newark and out. Less than twenty-four hours."

"No."

"If you want, your grandparents can see you. Maybe you do lunch downtown."

"I'm not going back to New York, Michael."

On the balcony, she dropped into a purple Adirondack chair. She put her feet on the rail.

"Pouting?"

"Don't tease. I can't believe you agreed to send me to New York."

Koons sat on the table. He put his hand on her wrist. "Sweetie..."

She stared at the sky. "You want me to go to the school where he killed her too?"

Koons sank. "I'm sorry, Isabel. I should've called you. I was thoughtless."

"You're not sorry." She turned to face him. "You're full of shit, Michael."

He shrugged. "I know. But it's fifty million dollars. It's go or no go. Tell me how to play you and I'll do it."

Isabel closed her eyes and brought her long fingers to her forehead. "You're not forgiven," she said finally.

13

Memphis PD knew Joe Blunt, and Sun Studio had video security and there was a traffic camera right there on Union Avenue, so Donnie Bliss's story was lining up right.

Sipp decided he'd go to see Lola Styles not at her place of business, what with tourists from the seven continents looking for the ghost of Elvis. Sipp's partner, Dee Milton, who had diabetes so bad they were going to take a foot, agreed the best approach was to see Lola Styles at home. But let's wait until Joe Blunt arrives.

Joe Blunt arrived at 10:38 p.m.

Sipp waited for Milton to make it up the last few stairs; then he knocked twice.

Lola Styles answered.

Sipp showed his badge.

She wore a loose lime blouse over black jeans and floppy socks, and over there sat Joe Blunt, his knitting needles clacking, rocking chair squeaking. Longneck empties stood on the end table.

A lifeless lava lamp sat on top of the silent TV. A crocheted throw in Titan blue and white was crumpled on the sofa. She retrieved it so the detectives could sit.

"You made that, Joe Blunt?" Sipp asked as she tossed it in a closet.

"Uh-huh," he replied. Clack clack. A squeak from the rocking chair, same as the one he kept in Tooley's bar.

Milton sat with an oomph. Two flights just about killed him.

"You want something to drink, Detectives?" Styles asked.

Later, Sipp would tell her she seemed awfully nervous.

"Thank you, but no."

"Just water for me," Dee Milton said, his stomach pouring over his belt.

Sipp waited while Milton replenished.

Then, tugging his Van Dyke, he said, "We're wanting to talk to you about Donald Harry Bliss. You know. Billboard Man?"

She sat in the old chair next to the TV. She couldn't help but look toward Joe Blunt. "All right. I mean, I sort of lost hope now. You know, the reward..."

"Mall food," muttered Dee Milton in disgust.

Over there: Clack. Squeak.

"That's a ways out of our jurisdiction, Miss Styles," Sipp said as he removed a PDA from his jacket pocket. "Detective Milton and I are investigating the death of a young man. Boone Stillwell. You said you saw Bliss arguing with Stillwell. Is that correct?"

She nodded. "I did."

Clack. Squeak.

"Where?"

She repeated the name of the street corner she reported to both the 888 number and the Memphis PD tip line.

"I see. Can I ask you how you knew it was Donald Harry Bliss?"

"I spoke to him at the studio," she said. She looked at Joe Blunt, who kept his head down, eyes on his work. "We had a drink later. Coincidence."

"All right," Sipp said. He typed with his thumb. "Now what about Stillwell? How did you know it was him?"

She hesitated. "I suppose I saw his picture in the paper."

Clack. Squeak.

As he dabbed his moist forehead with a handkerchief, Milton asked, "And which paper would that be, ma'am?"

"*The Commercial-Appeal*. What else?"

"Now, see, that's a problem right there, Miss Styles," Sipp said, "because the photo of Mr. Stillwell didn't appear in the newspaper or online until after you called."

Milton said, "Also, you know about the closed-circuit TV cameras on Union Avenue? Plus also at Sun? In the gift shop?"

Silence.

Staring at her, Joe Blunt said, "Did you fuck Stillwell too?"

She looked across the room in disbelief.

"Too?" asked Dee Milton.

"I guess she ain't told you she did him," Joe Blunt said. "Billboard Man."

"No..." said Sipp, who'd stopped thumb-typing. "Miss Styles?"

"I...We did spend some time together," she said slowly.

With a knitting needle, Joe Blunt pointed toward the bedroom. "You had them both in there?"

She said, "Joe...What are you doing, Joe?"

Joe Blunt looked over his shoulder at the detectives. "Maybe that's why they quarreled. Over Lola. The little fella and Billboard Man."

Sipp stood. Milton wriggled to the sofa's edge.

They invited Lola Styles to the police station.

Joe Blunt too.

"I don't think so," Joe Blunt said. "This is her business, not mine."

Clack. Squeak.

He heard a rap on the door.

"Hold on," he shouted. He was thinking about something else and was surprised, and more than a little bit disappointed, to find he was in Memphis.

He grabbed a towel and quickly dried his hair. It stood in spikes as he opened the door.

"I want—" Ginger Stillwell pulled back. "What in the world are you doing?"

"Trying to get the black out."

The towel was draped on his shoulders now. He wore jeans. No shirt, barefoot.

"With what?"

"Hot water. Cold water."

She returned from the laundry room with a little box of Tide.

Moments later, the sink overflowed with soap bubbles.

"It'll take a while, but it'll get it done."

He looked at himself in the mirror. He looked at her too.

"Don't get any ideas," she said.

"No ideas," he agreed as she pushed his head toward the sink.

Next morning, they were on President's Island, looking for the place the newspaper said Memphis PD found Boone's body.

Ginger had a map and a newspaper clipping in her lap. Bliss was driving a little car they' d rented off Beale Street. For a moment, he' d forgotten he could use his own name. Frank Niewidzialny, he' d almost said to the clerk. J.J. Walk. John Bleak.

"Who are you today?" Ginger whispered at the counter.

The late-morning air was thick. The sun was behind gray clouds, hiding as if it wasn't sure it wanted the day to begin. They could've used Boone's car, but somehow that seemed at least disrespectful and most likely macabre—driving it to find where he' d been dumped.

"Look for yellow tape," she said as they drove along.

"There's more to go," he said. "It's too residential here."

"We're going to go in deep, I guess."

Not too deep. A local would know where to bury a body so it would be found.

"I didn't think it was like this," she said as she kept a finger on the map.

"Built up."

"I was thinking wilderness." She looked around as they passed a glass-and-steel corporate park, its ample lot filled with cars. "Out of all of these people, you' d think somebody might've seen it."

Bliss pressed on, the curved road narrowing, and soon new homes and industry were behind them.

"This might be it," she said, tapping the map.

Agreeing, he pulled off the road.

He followed her into a patch of land dense with thick trees. She climbed over jutting roots. Then she waited as she came up on a fallen tree that had settled like a barricade.

"Up or under?" she asked.

He looked at the turf. If someone brought a body here, he didn't drag it.

He held out his hand to help her over.

From the other side, she did the same.

At a fork, they looked at each other.

"We could split up," she suggested.

He had his prepaid cell in his hand. "No bars."

"Let's go right."

He followed. His sleeves were rolled to the elbow. Hers too.

Forty-five minutes later and farther on down the road, they found yellow tape strung around the trunks of three trees. Inside the triangle was a shallow grave. No one had bothered to fill it up.

Ginger went under the tape and walked slowly to the grave's edge.

He held back, expecting tears and a prayer.

"The police—" She turned, thinking he was right there.

But he remained on the other side of the tape. He didn't know what she wanted. He wasn't sure why they were in the woods.

She walked toward him.

"Do you think they're done here?"

The police? No squad car. But the tape…He said, "I don't know."

"Either they forgot to take the tape down or they're coming back."

"For what?"

"To look for Ol' Buddy."

She turned to the grave's edge. He ducked under the tape.

"Ol' Buddy?" He imagined a dog lost in the woods, frightened at night, desperate for food.

"Boone's gun. His father gave it to him."

They stepped to the grave. "What kind?"

"I couldn't tell you. Except he said it had a pearl handle. I don't know if it was, but the handle was white."

He looked at the black soil.

"I told the cops back there that if they didn't find it, it meant the killer stole Ol' Buddy. I know that's so. I told them: Boone wouldn't let it go."

He nodded.

"Maybe he threw it into the woods."

Bliss said, "They looked, don't you think? The cops."

Ginger ran her fingers through her hair. She scratched the back of her neck. "I suppose. I need to look for myself. I owe him that much."

He said, "Let's see what we can find."

"Root around that way," she told him as she walked off.

With a flash of sunlight, the bar door swung open with a bang and Lola Styles charged past the pool table and flew at Joe Blunt, who had his head down. His rocking chair tipped over, and they both crashed to the floor, Joe Blunt's dragon beneath them. Lola Styles was on him, straddling his chest, punching and pounding at his face. Swearing and spitting.

Though the men cleared out to huddle by the open door, the mousy bartender watched with glee. She'd been hoping someone would kick the shit out of Joe Blunt for as long as she could remember. He bleeds and the drinks are on me, she thought.

"You son of a bitch" was the general tenor of Styles's complaint. "You cowardly bastard."

Soon it occurred to the bartender that Joe Blunt was letting her whale on him.

Sure enough, Joe Blunt was smiling.

Between chuckles, he said, "Hey, you just let me know when you tire out..."

In time, the blows slowed, and Lola Styles let out something between a cry and a sigh of resignation.

Joe Blunt wriggled free.

He stood, tugged on his nylon jacket and offered a hand to Styles, who was kneeling on dirty hardwood, her boot soles showing wear.

No one among the ragtags in the bar could recall ever seeing Lola Styles cry. But now she was sobbing. Her shoulders rattled.

"You son of a bitch," she moaned.

Joe Blunt's hand still hung in the air. "Come on now," he said kindly.

Eyes ringed red, she looked up.

Sagging, she took his hand.

The mousy bartender watched as Joe Blunt stepped aside to let Lola Styles exit before him.

Simpering, damp with sweat, she passed by.

And Joe Blunt reared and punched her in the back of the head. Lola Styles pitched forward, hit an empty bar stool and landed smack on the floor. Whether she lay still by choice or chance was impossible to tell.

Joe Blunt stared and none of the pointless men moved.

The mousy bartender, wet rag in hand, climbed onto the bar, then hopped down.

Joe Blunt retrieved his knitting bag.

On the way back, he nudged the bartender aside and lifted his girl by the belt and the back of her jeans.

Hauled her out into the humid Memphis afternoon, her arms dangling, back of her hands scraping sidewalk.

"Shara, what is it?"

Seymour Riegel's admin pulled him out of a partners' meeting. He hurried to his office: A call from his granddaughter—what could it mean?

"Are you all right?"

"I'm good, Zeyde. All good."

As he looked down on Park Avenue, Riegel smiled. His late mother tried to teach baby Shara to speak Yiddish, a then 90-year-old Polish émigré holding her 2-year-old great-granddaughter on her knee.

He sighed. "Shara…"

"I know." She was in her advisor's office at UCLA. The skanky British man who was looking for her was gone, her friends and coworkers said. It's safe, Isabel, probably. Or is it Shara now? "How's Bobeshi?"

"We're fine," Riegel replied. What can you say? Her burden was as heavy as theirs. For her, mother killed. For them, daughter. It was worse than either could've ever imagined. "Where are you?"

"In Los Angeles," she replied, "but I'm coming to New York."

"You are?" Down below, the leaves were clinging to the trees on the grassy islands. A cavalcade of taxis rushed uptown.

"Yeah, I'm surprised too. But it's a meeting. On Wall Street."

"For the picture?"

"Uh-huh."

As he sat, Riegel said, "How can I help, Shara?"

"Well, Zeyde, it's like this…"

14

He drove for hours to get to a branch of his bank, one that had offices on every other corner in New York City, but few in Tennessee or Mississippi.

He'd said, "I'm going for a drive."

She was upstairs in her room. They'd taken to using the hotel phone to speak to each other. No more knocking on the door, no more dropping by; last night, they ate in different places; they didn't know where the other one went. Ginger sent a text: Can you think of anything…?

It was dribbling to nothing now, the entire enterprise. They were wasting time. Boone was dead. The police had little to say. Bliss insisted he'd never been a cop. He had no idea how they worked. Maybe they were on it. Maybe they were circling in.

The Glock 17 she saw in his glove compartment? He tossed it in the Mississippi before he left for St. Louis.

"I'm going for a drive."

"Where to?" she asked. It was a sunny Friday morning.

"Little Rock."

"Arkansas?" Then she said, "Are you coming back?"

Yes.

"You don't have to."

Stillwell followed him to Memphis. If Stillwell stayed in Jerome, he'd be alive.

"I will. But can I say something?"

She was in a T-shirt and panties. Her window faced the sun. "Go ahead."

"You're not going to find Ol' Buddy. Not out there."

"No, I guess not."

"No more searching and digging. OK?"

He was going to suggest that she come along since Little Rock was on the way toward home. But he had no right. Maybe he should let her root around all she wanted to. Digging a hole: It was something.

They hadn't talked about it yet. Her husband killed. His wife killed. How do you cope?

"You OK for cash?" he asked.

"That was unnecessary, Donnie."

He'd given her $500. Enough to gas up Stillwell's car, spend a night or two in a motel.

She said, "I'm keeping receipts."

He was down to his last clean shirt. The rest were at a Chinese laundry.

"You'd better get going," she said. "If you're coming back."

He was hoping she'd realize she could be heartsick and guilt-ridden wherever she might go. He recalled they knew Ginger at the biker bar. She had a hometown. Cotillion and other friends.

Crossing into Arkansas, he looked down at his phone. Nobody called.

He let himself in and kicked the bed to wake her.

He was drinking paper-cup coffee and no, he didn't bring her none.

She mumbled out of a deep chemical sleep.

"Go away," she said through the haze. "Far."

"You're talking about it. Now."

Joe Blunt pulled back the sheet.

Naked on the bottom, some old spaghetti-strap thing on top. Elvis, of course. Shoplifted.

"You about broke my head, Joe," she said as she grabbed at the sheet.

"Yeah, but I didn't. Now let's go."

The scent of bleach clung to the steamy air. Joe Blunt looked toward the bathroom. "Maybe that was smart. Doing it again." That was as much as he was going to give her.

She sat up. "They're going to come here and spray that shit that shows blood."

"What makes you think they're so far along that you could be the killer?"

"Me, Joe? Man…I don't think so."

"Blood in your tub. Your sheet around the body."

She wobbled as she stood, steadying with fingers on the nightstand. She retrieved a kimono robe, red and scored with Japanese characters and prowling tigers and whatnot. A gift from Joe Blunt, who knows where he got it.

He followed her toward the bathroom. She sat on the toilet, gathering the robe to pee.

"Joe, I don't understand why you want to put us on the opposite side of this thing."

"I ain't in this thing, Lola."

She dabbed, flushed, then went for her toothbrush. "You ain't?"

"Plus if you got yourself out, there ain't no thing."

"Well, I guess we'll see."

"Yeah. It could go either way."

Toothbrush tucked in her cheek, she said, "Meaning what, Joe?"

"Word against word. But blood in your tub. Your sheet."

Your tire tracks, you dumb son of a bitch. Your hair, fiber, DNA, handprints, whatever the fuck on my bedding. Your rap sheet. You up in Brushy. Your history, you moron. You think you own me?

Maybe you left some of that five-pointed star that's on your fist on the kid's face when you punched him to death.

It had a light-rail system. River Rail. Blue line, green line. Fifteen stops. It crossed the Arkansas River, rattling along at a steady pace. He was eager to try it, to nestle in and forget.

He had a hell of a beef tenderloin sandwich for lunch. Sea-salt potato chips. Icy beer out of the bottle.

Scanning the menu, he tried to imagine which sandwich Pup would've ordered.

Not long ago, he could enter a restaurant and think of nothing but ticking time. The past gone, and no future. Now he was Donnie Bliss again. It was right there in front of him: Moira was dead and Pup would have nothing to do with him, and his life had been for nothing.

He moved $20,000 out of two growth funds and into checking. Three thousand dollars in $100 bills were in his sneakers now.

When he buried the money, he looked at the driver's license and library card he had in the name of Frank Niewidzialny of Miami, Missouri. He walked them toward a trash can at the curb, but then he put them in his pocket.

The taxi-yellow train rolled by.

Niewidzialny. Where did that come from?

He never did ask the U.S. marshals why they chose Jellico. Had Pup?

He took out his phone.

"Michael?"

"Sam, I can't. Not now."

Bliss wandered toward the rental car. He had a choice to make. "Any fallout?"

"We're aces, Sam. Please."

"What aren't you telling me?"

Koons stopped. The financials were spread across Sir Bernie's conference table, all collated and ready for presentation. He played with the numbers, tweaking them in his favor. Isabel would never know.

"Sam, I'm harried. It's Friday. Isabel is fine. It came, it went."

Not so. Here in Little Rock, the people at the bank knew he was Billboard Man. They peered around corners as he signed papers. Last night at a soul food place in Memphis, he thought he caught them staring. Maybe not. Maybe.

He had no one to answer to. It didn't matter. Pup had friends, classmates, professors, coworkers—a future.

They'll ask, but she won't explain. He could hear her: Yeah, it happens. No, my mom was great. A teacher, right. Sure I do. Sure I miss her. Thanks.

Pup, inscrutable. Deliberately vague. Above it. Clear.

But later, when she was alone. Pup, frowning, trying to put it in place. Hurting.

She was like that from the moment she was born: At some point, she was unreachable. Nobody knew. A mystery.

"Two mysteries," Moira had said. "The two of you."

"Michael—"

Koons said, "If I had something to tell you, I would."

No, I don't think you would.

"Sam, I'm sorry, really, but I'm at something here." A $50 million deal. The one to put me right where I want to be.

"Is she all right? Say it."

"She's fine." He tapped the Bluetooth headset, cutting the link.

Standing there in Little Rock.

Bliss took the paperback out of his rear pocket and tossed it onto the passenger's seat.

He punched in his father's number at the ranch, the same one they had when he was a boy.

"Pa, it's—"

The old man hung up.

Bliss took comfort in that. Had something happened to Pup, his father would've blasted him with blame.

Goldsworthy was done. He knew it. Outplayed. Never mind the bollocks about the end is nigh. The end was right fuckin' here, mate.

Remembering, sitting with a mole in Belfast as the Troubles wound down, Imperial Stout at the elbow, O'Gara his name was, and O'Gara said, "When I go, I'm taking them with me." "Them" being everyone, seeing as how the Irish hated him for being born in Blackpool and the Brits did as well for his red hair, fair skin and native ways. Full of talk he was, O'Gara. They found him with his tongue cut out, the tongue itself nailed to a post above the body.

Defeated, Goldsworthy now took to the coast highway. He saw a family of deer grazing in a Pacific Palisades park, a doe and two fawns. He walked woozy toward them, saying, "Your dad's a hat rack now." They looked at him, their dark eyes saying he wasn't worth the trouble of bounding away, even when he flicked a cigarette at them.

Later, shoes hooked to a finger, pants rolled to the calves, he cruised the beach. At sunset, a lean, well-tanned man in a marble-sack swimsuit looked him over and then strolled to the public toilets. Goldsworthy followed, a distant stirring in his loins. I've got a bit of worth, he thought. Without a word, the pretty man reached for the Brit's belt buckle. As Goldsworthy closed his eyes and leaned against the cinder-block wall, the man reared back and slammed his forehead against Goldsworthy's nose. He punched Goldsworthy in the stomach, the uppercut lifting Goldsworthy off his sandy feet. Gasping for air, Goldsworthy fell to his knees, his skull bleeding. The man reached into his swimsuit, produced his cock, spread his legs and pissed on him.

The man left the cash and credit cards, but he took the knife and sheath Goldsworthy wore around his neck. And his shoes. He took Goldsworthy's shoes.

Piss-soaked, Goldsworthy sat with his back to the wall, blood seeping from his nose, his silver hair a grotesque frame about his throbbing face, aware it had all come to this. He leaned his shoulders against the wall to stand. He wanted to see himself, but the mirror above the sink was a pie tin.

He stumbled out of the bunker and into darkness. Way over there, a boy was flying a kite, running with glee to keep it in the air.

Goldsworthy walked toward the pounding ocean.

"Fuck it," he said.

On my own terms.

Soon the water was up to his knees.

The waves knocked him back as he pressed on.

He wasn't going to swim. No, he was going out on his feet.

A big roaring wave clapped down on him, knocking him under, filling his lungs with salt water.

Goldsworthy scrambled to stand upright. But another wave sent him under again.

He struggled to breathe. He coughed. Water stung his injured nose.

Another wave pitched him toward the beach.

Goldsworthy began to paddle, riding the surf, retreating, the waves nudging and bobbing him along.

On his feet again, water to his knees, he walked to the sand. He collapsed.

Crawled into a ball, he woke up shivering, a Jeep's headlights drawing near. "On your feet," the cop said through a bullhorn.

Goldsworthy complied.

Later, after the cops sent him on his way, Goldsworthy remembered O'Gara. The bastard had it right. When you go, take them with you. All of them.

If you can't get them all, get the right one. The one that hurts the most.

"When is something going to happen?"

"I don't know. It may not."

"Then I'm supposed to limp off and go back home?"

Yes.

"I've got a lot of time invested in this."

Time. It means nothing to memory.

"I' d at least like to know why."

He sipped his beer. Soul music blared; the singer sold it like he' d die if he didn't.

Ginger Stillwell: "One question: Why kill him?"

I don't know.

"To what end?"

He wasn't much of a listener—for the past few years, when people talked to him, he wasn't listening at all—but he was trying to suss out if there was a way to get her going back to Jerome with a semblance of pride. It wasn't her fault. None of it.

"You know, the Boone you saw. That was all show. All show. I've seen him puff up before and the boys would pull him away, his bony arms flailing, and that's how it would end. This time..."

The waitress circled. Best BBQ in Memphis? I don't know about that. But it was fine. He looked over his shoulder. If she needed the table, he would've suggested they move on. But the dinner rush was gone. People had settled in. Right now, nobody was looking at Billboard Man.

Ginger picked at the last of the cornbread. "This time, I went too far."

He told himself to stay still. Sip the beer, but don't empty the bottle.

"I mean, really. Were you going to sweep me off my feet, put me on a white horse and ride me off to a castle in the sky? Were you there to save me? I mean, what exactly is wrong with me?"

He said, "Nothing."

"I could give you a list."

"Nothing."

"Then why am I in Memphis, Tennessee, on a Saturday night with a man who can't bear my company—"

"I can bear your company," he said. "That's not it."

"—and I'm on a fool's errand." She sat back, shook her head, raised her hand. "And now look at me: A couple, three beers and I'm a fountain of self-pity. Is there much worse?"

Than self-pity?

The waitress offered two more longnecks.

He asked for the check.

Ginger opened her pocketbook.

"It's on me," he said as he extended a leg to dip into the pocket of his jeans.

"Either way," she said. "The only money I have is yours."

He peeled off twenties he'd drawn at the bank.

She still had her hand in her bag. When she withdrew it, she was holding a shot glass.

"I was hoping to bring home Ol' Buddy. Instead I'm bringing this."

With a flick of his fingers, he asked her to pass it over.

The shot glass wore the Sun Studio logo. A black-vinyl disk ringed in yellow, a guitar in the middle.

"Where did you get it?"

"The cops. It was in Boone's car."

He turned it over. A price sticker was on the bottom.

She leaned her elbows on the plastic tablecloth. "What?"

"Any idea where he bought this?"

She said no. If there was a receipt, the cops hadn't found it. She said, "What are you thinking?"

15

They met in the lobby. Guests checking out, morning sunlight pouring in.

"Tell me right now: How stupid was I last night?"

He smiled. "Not very."

"Did we…?"

"Not even a little."

"My head is pounding."

After a double bourbon nightcap, I guess so.

"I don't know what I'm doing."

He asked if she wanted breakfast.

"I' d better."

Then they drove over to Sun Studio.

She hesitated at the door. He bought two tickets. He thought to ask for Lola Styles. But not yet.

See. Right there. X marks the spot. Where Elvis stood when he sang.

A fat guy weighed in, said he drove all the way from Vermont. He wanted to share. "Here's where he came when he asked to see Sam Phillips," he said, pointing. "To make a little record for his mama. See, the secretary's name plaque is still on the desk."

Ginger leaned toward Bliss. "Boone must've been in heaven," she whispered.

"I'll be back in a minute," he said. He held up the shot glass.

When he returned, he found she'd been crying. She turned away, facing old microphone stands and cables.

"He bought it here," he said. "The same sticker."

"We could've guessed he was here," she said as the tissue went back in her bag. "He wouldn't have passed up the opportunity."

They stepped into the sunlight beyond the green awning.

"The tour guide," he said. "He would've seen her. She would've seen him."

She stopped. "The woman you were with…"

"When was he here? Can you piece it together?"

"We could ask them at the hospital when they let him out."

He nodded. "Can you make a log of his calls?"

She dipped into her handbag.

A tour bus eased in front of them, the air brakes wheezing. The door opened.

Bliss reached for her elbow. If they were going to work it out now and give it to the cops, they ought to step aside and get out of the pedestrian flow.

But then he heard tires squeal, and he pulled her close.

A red Ford pickup careened in front of the tour bus, stopping abruptly at an angle to the curb. If the bus had been moving, the Ford would've cut it off dead, risking an accident. But now the bus was standing still. There was no point.

Bliss crouched to look.

Lola Styles was in the passenger's seat.

She turned to say something to the driver.

Ignoring her, the man scowled.

She shook her head.

Now Ginger Stillwell was looking at the red truck too. She said, "What's he so mad about?"

The door opened and Lola Styles jumped out, her face knit in disgust.

Then she saw Bliss. She sprang tall in shock.

She spun on a boot heel and pounded the pickup's door with the flat of her hand.

The scowling man in the muscle shirt leaned over and pushed open the door. She climbed back inside.

Bliss watched.

Lola Styles spoke.

The big scowling man with the widow's peak looked past her. He looked at Bliss.

She pointed west on Union Avenue. Drive, she told him.

The man hardened his glare. Buffing up, he continued to scowl.

Bliss looked at him, thoughts muting his expression.

Lola Styles shouted. She smacked the dashboard.

The big scowling man lifted his foot off the brake. He rolled a tire up on the sidewalk. He bounced the truck down off the curb, all the while staring at Bliss.

Then they drove off.

A group of Japanese tourists flowed from the bus.

"That her?" Ginger Stillwell asked.

Bliss nodded, his eyes on the truck.

Uneventful flight. Koons was perplexed: Why go a day early if you don't want to go at all? But she insisted. She said, "I'm going on Saturday. You can hang back if you want." He should've asked why, but with Isabel Jellico, answers tended to conceal more than reveal.

First-class amenities made him smile. Champagne or mimosa? Salmon or beef medallions? A second serving of profiteroles, Mr. Koons? A foot massage?

Next year at this time, Sir Bernie's private jet would be at his disposal. He'd be handling A-list talent. A table at Melisse. An upgrade to a Ferrari or maybe a vintage Bentley. Pharmaceutical grade—No. But a second home in Cabo, surely.

She slept with her hoodie up. It covered her cropped hair, the string pulled tight around her face.

Koons had friends in Manhattan, a few in Brooklyn. He said she could come with. Join us, Isabel. Get outside yourself. Broadway, dinner. They say there's a club on the West Side that brings Ibiza right to New York City. You can dance through the night.

You don't actually want me to come, do you, Michael?

"No thanks," she said, "but you go ahead. I've got assignments, a few papers to write." She was adapting Malamud in Screenwriting 302.

They were in a cookie-cutter suites hotel on the airport property.

"Are you sure? I hate to..."

You see me as someone who dances through the night? "Have a blast, Michael. Really."

She headed for the shower.

At 7:30 a town car picked her up and drove her to a Spanish restaurant a few miles away.

She would've bet she could remember everything about life in and around New York, from the moment her memory reel began until the day the U.S. marshals shipped them to Appleyard, Washington.

Yet she forgot to bring a jacket. She had the hoodie zipped to her chin, her hands in its pouch.

"Turn up the heat, please," she said to the driver as she put her laptop bag at her feet.

Her grandparents were waiting in the vestibule.

"Shara," her grandfather said, his face awash with sympathy.

Her tiny grandmother reached up to stroke her cheek. "Sy, look how tall she is."

The maître d' waited as she lifted the strap of her scruffy laptop bag over her head. A private table was reserved.

"You're shivering," her grandfather said.

"I left my jacket at home."

"You'll take my mink," her grandmother insisted.

They laughed. The idea of Shara in mink…

The maître d' led them through the crowded restaurant, past red banquettes and dark wood; tapas with chorizo, plump olives, grilled octopus; thick steaks and rich *garnacha* from Priorat decanted in crystal. A woman played flamenco guitar.

Shara's back to the wall, a round table. Each grandparent held a hand.

Smiling sheepishly, she looked at the empty fourth seat.

Hi, Mom. Moira smiled. Hi, baby. I miss you. Me too, Mommy.

"Did you bring…?"

"Seymour," Evelyn Riegel scolded.

He knew were it not for business, Shara would be back in Los Angeles.

She unzipped the laptop bag. "Here," she said as she passed him a copy of the financials. She'd taken it from Koons's carry-on as he slept in flight. He had no idea she'd stirred.

Riegel brought out his bifocals.

"Shara," her grandmother said, "do you hear from your father?"

Riegel looked at his wife.

She said, "Is it time to forgive? I only ask."

"Evelyn, please."

"He calls, Bobeshi," Shara replied as she gazed at the empty chair.

He'd bought a yellow pad at the 7-Eleven. She had several pens in her purse. They worked in her room. It was fine. The furthest thing.

"You haven't mentioned your daughter," Ginger said.

I haven't mentioned anything.

"It must have been awful."

"The timeline," he said, tapping the pad with a Jerome Utilities pen.

Past sunset, Memphis lights flickered, reflected off the silent TV. They ordered Chinese food. You wouldn't think it could taste so good, but why not? When the Chinese came, they only set up in New York and San Francisco? Ginger said they had a good Chinese place in Jerome. The owners' two little girls sat in the sun after pre-K and shucked peas.

White cartons and discarded napkins spilled out of the trash can.

"Did you call about his mail?"

"No phone bill yet," she said. "We'll have to go with what's on my cell."

Stillwell had called her several times before he was killed. The next to last time he'd said, "Come on, Ginger. Don't you know what's happening? This is the ticket. The ticket."

Within the half hour, Stillwell called again. "Ginger, now you listen. I am telling you we have got to move on this thing. What we have is real, legitimate information."

She said it had to be his last call. The sad truth was that it was unlikely he'd call anyone else. The ticket he'd talked about was the reward for finding Billboard Man.

"I know you've resisted," Bliss said, "but I think you've got to kick this to the police."

She was seated barefoot on the bed. He sat with his back to the desk.

She said, "Boone went to Sun Studio and bought a shot glass. That's a fact. The rest…"

"Let them put it together. Then go home."

She bristled, but then sagged.

"You've done all you could."

"Which is what?"

He shrugged. Who knew what the cops could do with technology? Not long ago, Bliss was told a man named Francis Cherry could locate him via GPS no matter where he went. Maybe the cops could find out where Stillwell was when he made those calls to Ginger.

"Kick it to the cops," he said.

"You yourself said it had to be Boone and this tour guide Lola."

No I didn't. Bliss stood. He stepped to gather the trash, stuffing the cartons into the plastic lining.

She said, "I don't know how, but they came together once they knew there was a reward."

"Ginger, I don't—"

A knock on the hotel room door.

Ginger bounced off the bed.

She said, "Did you tip the delivery guy?"

Bliss came up behind her, trash bag in his hand.

She looked through the peephole.

She opened the door.

Two girls, maybe 13 or 14 years old. “Is he Billboard Man?”

Ginger turned to him.

The girls giggled.

Bliss heard himself say, “Beat it.”

“He is. He surely is,” said the one with braces.

Bliss reached over Ginger’s shoulder to close the door.

The other girl raised her cell phone and snapped a photo.

Still giggling, the girls ran off.

Ginger stepped into the hall to watch them disappear.

“Beat it?” she asked. “How did they—”

“They were in the lobby when I asked the desk clerk about a Chinese place.”

Door closed, she joined him, filling up the shopping bag with plastic utensils, soy sauce packets, unused chopsticks. “That photo is going up on the Web, you know.”

“You’ d better hope Cotillion doesn’t see it,” he said.

“Why—Oh shoot. You’re in my room.”

Bliss took the shopping bag. The trash was going into a bin by the snack machine. No sense leaving her with the lingering scent of moo shu pork, lemon chicken and starchy rice.

Alone in the boiler room, Koo Young-Soon heard his laptop ding. Having drifted to sleep, he waited until the sound repeated to be sure he hadn’t imagined it.

Ding.

He stood, stretched, bent to the waist and looked at the message.

He clicked the link.

A photo had been posted in Flickr. “Billboard Man Hooking Up!!!” was the caption. The account belonged to someone in

Lenox, Tennessee. The photo was time stamped. Ninety-seven minutes ago.

He sat again to look closely at the screen.

The man in the photo looked like the drawing Mr. Cherry had ordered: an older version of the man in the photos that had been in the *Daily News* and the *Post* earlier in the week after the billboard stunt. Ones taken years ago outside a courthouse in Foley Square after his wife had been killed.

Koo moved the new photo to a facial-recognition program. Seconds later, it confirmed the visual match.

Donald Harry Bliss. He was still in Tennessee.

As instructed, Koo Young-Soon went to the phone.

"Happy Saturday night, Mr. Koo," Francis Cherry said. "Where are you?"

"In the bunker," he replied.

Cherry wore a white robe made of bamboo terry, the word *Dignity* embroidered in gold at the breast. "Such dedication. You will be going places. Though not tonight."

Saturday night. Tuesday night. Thursday. It mattered not to Koo Young-Soon, who kept hidden a deep secret: He preferred the company of his own active imagination. In the world of his handheld multiplatform gaming system, Koo was emperor of Xophylia Prime and husband to Gx, goddess of destiny, who took on physical form only when Mzyop approached the 13th house. Which would be in about 11 minutes, once he released the Pause button.

Meanwhile, Cherry was in Potentate Suite in the Trump Soho with that ditzy girl from the bowling alley and her mother, a dead ringer for post-Hitchcock Tippi Hedren. The girl's idiocy was an act. She graduated from Barnard and worked in research at an oil company's New York office. Now between official posts, Mom had been a deputy ambassador to Tonga under Clinton. Tonight, they were in separate bedrooms, unaware of each other's presence.

Mom had held up versus time; naked, she had at least as much to offer as her issue, who was too young to know that what she had wasn't all that until she could advance it with a twist. The two women had the same freckle below the navel. Cherry had yet to choose. Right now, he was thinking he'd have them rush nude into the living room at the same time to answer an emergency. Whoops, he would say.

Koo: "Bliss is still in Tennessee."

"Is he now?"

Cherry sat on the bed. The daughter, who was wearing as a headband a tie he bought on the street for $3, knelt behind him to nibble on his ear.

"Are his bags packed?" he asked.

"It's impossible to say."

"So he doesn't know. Blabberdashery. Et cetera."

"I could guess, Mr. Cherry."

Cherry looked over his shoulder. "Does he know?" he whispered to her.

The girl shrugged. Then she dipped for Cherry's neck.

"Anything else?"

Koo said, "It appears he's in a hotel room with a woman."

"Well, I'll be. The lone wolf keeps racking 'em up. How many hotels in Memphis, Mr. Koo?"

"Many."

"Start dialing. Just in case."

"Yes, sir."

"And repost the photo on whateverdotcom. Hit the honey hive. Buzz, buzz."

Joe Blunt cupped his chin in his hand, Lola Styles asleep over there on the sofa or maybe just drowsing bare-assed, blue tat to the ceiling. Up on the kitchen table, the laptop's screen light shone on his face, his unruly eyebrows, V-shaped as he frowned, and also his widow's peak, Joe Blunt in otherwise darkness, killing a Memphis Saturday night, his knitting bag at his knee. In the tin ashtray, a cigar wrapper loosely packed with second-rate pot was down to a nub. Joe Blunt sighed in boredom.

The Web wasn't good for much other than porn and photos of bodies dismembered in accidents, war, terror and whatnot, but tonight he clicked away, the words in the search engine nothing more than *Billboard Man* and *Memphis*.

He pushed his knitting needles aside and slid the mouse. Click. Same old bullshit wire-service story 40, 50 times in newspapers and on TV across the United States.

Slid the mouse. Click. Same shit.

He thought about getting up and wobble-walking all of 6 feet to retrieve another cold beer from the fridge.

By the time he returned, the screen was blank.

Sat. Slid mouse. Replenished the search engine. Click.

Wha—Hold on. Hold on.

Click.

A photo filled the screen.

He sat up.

"Lola," he shouted as he toggled the mouse. "Lola!"

She turned over, sat upright. Whoa. Cheap shit or not, the pot knocked her silly.

She slap-padded barefoot across hardwood, Roy Orbison on her bleach-stained T.

"Look." Joe Blunt pointed.

She leaned in. Squinted.

"That's them," she said.

"Says here it was taken tonight."

"Could be so. Same clothes as today."

Son of a bitch Bliss has his arm around that chick.

Joe Blunt stood, stepped around his knitting bag. "I know that hotel," he said. "The numbers on the doors."

"You want me along?"

"Fuck no." He grabbed up his dragon jacket. "He's mine."

They rode in silence, nestled in the limo's plump leather seats, each adrift and deep in thought. Seymour Riegel squeezed the bridge of his nose. He let out a long sad breath.

"She's not much like Moira, though," his wife said.

The driver pressed toward the Lincoln Tunnel. The inbound upper ramp crowded to a standstill. The majesty of the Manhattan skyline reflected in the black river water.

"No," Riegel replied. Every life is a series of milestones, great, good and bad. But none matches the birth and death of a child. Those are the only markers between sentience and eternity. "Her hands and fingers, maybe; a few gestures. The way she pauses to think."

"They were regular buddies. Shara and him."

Riegel hadn't approved of Donnie Bliss. He expected more for his only child: a man who matched her in education and, God forgive my arrogance, in pedigree. Then here comes a mystery man, California calm, a life on the road, tumbleweed, easy charm, windswept hair, long slow strides, the warm smile, even the scar near his eye. Nothing planned: no strategy, no expectations. For the life Moira saw for herself—and let's be honest here, it wasn't what Riegel would've preferred, teaching in that rundown school in the Bronx, abandoning their old family friends, new traditions, no traditions, the crazy apartment—Bliss was perfect. She was in love, deeply and thoroughly. Riegel knew why: For both, they were the other, the opposite. The attraction was undeniable.

It was preordained. New worlds appeared whenever they were together.

Why did he do it? What did Moira lack? It was inconceivable that she should have to win him back, this man of no ambition, of no acclaim.

"Sometimes I can't remember why you hate him," Evelyn Riegel said evenly.

Riegel didn't reply.

"Was it really his fault?"

The car inched ahead.

She said, "I think she needs him. Our Shara."

Again, silence.

"Sy?"

"You may be right," he said finally.

"He was a good father."

"He was," Riegel allowed.

16

He knew how to take care of himself. Or so he thought. Life on the road taught him the hard way, but it stuck. Once he slept near the old Rock Island line tracks in central Oklahoma. He was rolled in a ball, using a hardcover book as a pillow. The fire he built had gone out. A man came up and tried to rustle his backpack. Donnie Bliss had a rusted railroad-tie spike in his fist. From his knees, he punched the hunched-over man above the ear. The man went facedown into the tall grass. Bliss was 16 years old.

But earlier this year he had taken a bad beating. He hadn't seen it coming. He was distracted. Maybe he wanted to be put down for good. The man beat him with a sap and hurt him as deep and as often as he wanted to. It took John Bleak a while to recover. John Bleak had to dip himself in ice baths to stop the swelling. John Bleak had to pay cash to have his mouth repaired, and now Donnie Bliss had new scars.

Nobody was going to come at him from nowhere again.

He excused himself, went up to his room and made several phone calls.

Ginger, he said when he returned, here's what you do…

He told her to move on to a new hotel, one out on the highway. Upscale: all glass and steel. They're expecting Mrs. Frank Niewidzialny of Miami, Missouri.

Take the credit card. Go on.

Settle in.

Text me the room number.

"What's going on?" she asked as he watched her stuff her bag.

There's a car service waiting downstairs for you.

"Did something happen?"

Walk across the lobby. Don't stop.

"Are we in danger?"

"I'll come," he said as he put her in the elevator.

Suitcase at her side, Ginger Stillwell sank into herself as the doors sealed shut.

Joe Blunt didn't know where the hotel was where Bliss and his girl were photographed. He was always saying shit like that, coming on with authority, a bully through and through. Because nobody told him, he didn't realize people knew he was an asshole. He thought he had everybody fooled.

He did figure out that the hotel was somewhere downtown and not a fine old establishment like the Peabody, stately brick, marble columns, wood trimming and such. Billboard Man's hotel was one of those prefab jobs they deliver on flatbed trucks and offer rooms at a discount. He could tell by the cheap fireproof door.

He'd bought 4,700 oxy tablets, 20 milligrams, in a room just like it, the woman who sold it to him done up and hair sprayed like she was hosting the *Today* show. She spread her legs just so and Joe Blunt saw she had a skinning knife Velcroed to her thigh.

Joe Blunt dipped into his dragon jacket and showed her the stock of a sawed-off double-barrel shotgun he' d tucked inside.

The same shotgun he carried now. He had Billboard Man's hotel room number in his head.

He started driving. At each hotel he parked the Ford pickup behind the hotel on the street or at its loading dock. He put that sawed-off inside his dragon jacket and made sure it was covered right. Then he hurried around the corner, entered the hotel with a purpose, took the elevator up, walked to the door with the number that was in the photo. Even though the number didn't exactly match the style or placement of the one he saw, he knocked.

"Open up," said Joe Blunt.

Four hotels, none containing Billboard Man in Room 632. Two no answers, probably out doing up Beale Street. One gray hair was in his shorts and not too pleased to be disturbed. One young couple toasted, the floor littered with empties, and she's over there in a bra and panties when Joe Blunt elbowed in to see if Billboard Man had gone and made it a party.

Fifth hotel. He parked, jumped out.

He disappeared around the corner.

Up the block, away from the streetlights, Donnie Bliss stepped out of his rental car. He carried a washcloth he' d taken from the room upstairs. He walked directly to the scowling man's Ford pickup, popped the hood, looked in and pulled out the clutch sensor. Burying it in his back pocket, he shut the hood and wiped away his prints, dirtying the hell out of the white cloth.

Then he went back toward the rental and waited for scowling man to appear.

He watched as Joe Blunt took a sawed-off shotgun out of his jacket and stowed it across the passenger's seat.

The truck engine wouldn't turn over.

The scowling man kept pumping and trying, but then he stomped out of the truck, slamming the door so hard it boomed and echoed. Furious, he looked this way, that way. He took out a cell phone, but he didn't use it.

He opened the hood. A few seconds passed and then he saw what had been taken.

In the car, Bliss had ducked out of sight. He had his foot ready to kick open the door when the scowling man arrived. He wished he'd had that Glock 17 he'd tossed.

Bliss rose slowly. He peered over the padded dashboard and saw Joe Blunt walking down the center of the back alley toward bright lights a few blocks away.

Bliss sat tall and drove off toward the river and the old Biloxi Box Company. They were the only landmarks he could recall from the night he spent with Lola Styles. It took him a while, up and down side streets, but he found what he thought was her building. Yeah, it was her building. He made note of the address.

Then he lit out for the highway.

"I can't say I'm not surprised," Ginger Stillwell said as he entered. "I had you halfway to somewhere else."

Without a word, Bliss turned into the bathroom, sealed the door, undressed, stepped into the shower, standing still as the water warmed. His fresh shirts were in his room downtown; so were his last pair of jeans. He was going to have to get back into dirty clothes. He needed to shave, but he didn't have his toiletry bag at hand, his preferred shaving cream and blade. He'd left two books behind too.

He wiped the steam off the mirror. He looked at himself.

Billboard Man.

"Refreshed?" Ginger asked. Barefoot, jeans, billowy aubergine blouse.

"We've got to go," he said as he sat on the king bed to tie his sneaker.

"I was hoping to luxuriate in this room until morning." She stood next to him.

He hated hotel rooms, even one as spacious and well designed and high in the sky as the room they'd given the Niewidzialnys of Miami, Missouri.

They put mints on the pillows.

"The man who pulled up in front of Sun Studio is looking for us," he said.

"Why?"

She dropped a hand on his shoulder.

I don't know.

"Donnie, why?"

He stood. "I say we kick this to the cops."

"You already said that, though."

He said, "It's a different thing now."

"How so?"

"Go home, Ginger."

"You think that man wants to hurt me?"

"I don't know what he wants." He reached, took her arms and slid his hands to hold hers. "You did what you could. I don't see how you could've done more."

She looked up.

"It doesn't feel right," she said. "It's not finished."

"It's time to grieve."

He held her. He didn't know if she could bear to press against him, the grime in his shirt, the kind of man he was.

"Good Lord," she said as she stepped back. "Who would've thought you'd turn out to be a friend?"

Detective Milton was so disheveled he might as well have stayed in his pajamas, his gangrenous foot like that, and he was eating a pastry the length of his arm, flakes falling like snow. Sipp, though, he was neat in seersucker, and he kept running his thumb and forefinger along his gray tie so it lined up right.

Paper cups of coffee on the conference room table. Powdered creamer.

Not yet 6 o'clock. The detectives heard next to nothing they didn't know. Was it worth coming in before dawn? If it helps her decide to get up and go…

But you had to give it to them, Sipp thought. When you consider she and her friend over there hadn't seen Sun's security tapes, probably didn't know Joe Blunt's history, hadn't seen Lola Styles [illegible] almost exactly where Mrs. Stillwell was now, Lola on th[illegible] tipping and giving it up, they did all right, the wife [illegible]nd over there.

[illegible] ain't nothing.

[illegible] coated in dust.

Sipp said, "You're saying he came after you."

Bliss said, "He came to the hotel."

Yawning, Milton said, "Because he saw this photo you mentioned."

Bliss nodded. Mrs. Stillwell nodded.

"Though you don't know that to be so," Sipp said, fingering his tie bar.

"The hotel has security cameras in the elevators," Bliss said.

"And we told you he saw us outside the record studio," Ginger added.

"Nah," Milton said as he lifted the pastry. "I'm hearing coincidence."

Bliss stood.

So Ginger did too.

Chomp. Milton.

Sipp said, "I suppose you're heading home for a funeral, Mrs. Stillwell."

She said it again: "It doesn't feel right to me."

Now Sipp was standing too.

Seated, Milton dabbed at the corners of his lips. "And what about you, Billboard Man?"

Bliss stepped away and held the door for Ginger.

Out on Union Avenue, the humidity already elbowing in, he said, "You can fly home."

She knew he agreed with the detectives. She was dismissed. "I' d like to bring Boone's car back. I'll feel better for it."

He faced the dull morning sun. "You're up for the drive?"

She nodded.

They walked toward his rental car. They rode in silence to the pound.

Outside the gate, she said, "I'm going to pay you back every cent I owe you."

"Put it toward the funeral," he replied.

After a moment or two, she said, "Well, I guess this is it."

She went to her toes to kiss his cheek.

"Thank you."

He nodded.

"Well…Good-bye, then."

Good-bye.

She walked toward the guard booth.

Bliss put the rental car in reverse. He drove downtown.

Back to the hotel. Back up to his room.

He shaved. He showered.

Soon he slept. On the floor this time, feet toward the door, but he allowed himself a pillow.

He sat up with a start. Maybe he should've followed her to the highway. Maybe that thug was on her tail.

He stared at the ceiling, hands cupped behind his head.

Took him a while to remember it wasn't his business.

He was going to go back to Carbondale and do it again. Rewind and then disappear.

Soon, despite the vacuum cleaner's hum in the hallway, he fell back to sleep.

Ginger Stillwell centered herself for the 20-plus-hour drive. She figured she' d stop in Oklahoma City for lunch, call Cotillion to tell her she was coming home, maybe Johnny Eagle too and plead for her job, and then devise a plan on where to spend the night, somewhere east of Albuquerque, maybe Amarillo, considering she hardly slept last night. Would it be so awful to use the credit card he gave her, the one with the name Niewidzialny on it?

Yes, it would be. Besides, I have enough money for a night in a motel, she thought as she reached into the glove compartment, fishing for music, Boone's car pep-pepping along in the slow lane on Route 40, her companion for the next 460 miles or so.

Hank Williams III. The CD she found.

All right, Hank. Show me what you got.

No, never mind.

Plugging in any of Boone's music was going to make it like he was sitting next to her, spewing philosophy, pointing out how Hank III was right on it, he had his finger on the pulse of the American people. Heir not only to his granddaddy but to Merle and Mr. Johnny Cash.

"And what, Boone? You don't think people in, I don't know, Norway have feelings about love and their family and neighbors and hard work?"

Ah, Boone. Goddamn it.

You child.

You sweet, dumb, lost child.

She shook her head.

Men.

Cars and trucks blew by. Abrupt wind across the plains puckered through the loose-fitted windows. She held the wheel with two hands.

A steady pace now, the sun on the washed-out, mud-brown road. She fell deep into memory, remembering the hopeful days.

Maybe she never did love him in her soul; maybe she never did think he was the only one on the planet, the one God sent across the universe to make her whole and complete. But she tried to love him through and through, and she did love him. He had his qualities.

Devotion was one of them.

And when he was lying in that hospital bed, 1,400 miles from his home, not sure whether his appendix might explode, what was I doing?

Counting tips.

Waiting for my white knight.

I let you down, Boone, didn't I?

She was crying steadily now.

Couldn't come through for you when you needed me most.

Even after you were gone I let you down.

Up ahead, an exit-only lane. She eased over.

Came around and got back on 40 going east.

Back to Memphis.

17

Modulating her voice, Mrs. Brent asked Estelle Negron to greet the appointees when they arrived. "Settle them in Mr. Cherry's office, if you would be so kind." An eager Negron agreed. There was no task Mr. Cherry could require that she would not endeavor to achieve to a state beyond perfection: The man had guaranteed her children's futures. God bless you, Mr. Cherry, she thought often; San Juan Bautista, watch over Mr. Francis Cherry. She said thank you several times to her benefactor—more than several, in fact. ("That's enough, dear," advised Mrs. Brent.) As for Cherry, he couldn't figure out why Mrs. Brent's little brown assistant was glowing, smiling and bobbing all the goddamned time, but what the hell. As long as we have peace.

Mrs. Brent was off to deliver the morning's *Journal* to a coffee baron from Cameroon who was in the conference room at the far end of the floor. The high commissioner for the Faroe Islands was in another, bearing high-tech snowshoes as a gift for Cherry. Both were scheduled for 8 a.m. meetings, as were the visitors who had yet to—

Security called. "Thank you. You may send them up," said Mrs. Brent, as stylish now as when she was the belle of the Morgan Bank.

Modeling her boss, Negron was dressed peppy in a gray suit and navy-blue shoes that matched her scarf. She stood by the elevator.

The door opened.

In a hoodie and cargo pants, Shara Bliss stepped out first, beverage in hand. She looked around: dark wood, sumptuous carpeting, chandeliers, Remington's cowboys on horses, Degas's ballerina, a miniature version of Rodin's *Burghers of Calais.* Encased in glass, an old-fashioned stock ticker. She wandered toward it. It had belonged to Charles Dow and Edward Jones.

Negron looked at the older man in gray pinstripe. "Mr. Koons?" she asked.

The little man in blue and mauve said, "I'm Michael Koons."

"Seymour Riegel," the older man said. "Miss Bliss's attorney."

Shara Bliss turned. She smiled. "Sorry," she said to Negron. "Pretty sweet, this place."

"I have an appointment with Mr. Cherry," Koons said as he stepped toward the admin. "My client and I."

"And my grandpops," said Shara Bliss, pointing with her thumb.

Mmmm, thought Negron, whose street savvy was honed to a pinprick. I would like to be in that room to see what this girl has in mind. She's nervous, but that little man in light purple, he's too stressed to notice. The older guy, he's sitting tight. He's done this downtown thing before.

"Follow me, please," said Estelle Negron.

Koons had been knotting his tie when he'd heard a knock on his hotel room door. Room service? Did I…He'd gotten back to Newark at a little after 4 a.m. What a night. High times. He wouldn't want to live in New York City, but what a hard-core party town. Behind the dirt and grime, it was Magicland. And discreet? My goodness. He could still feel the music pounding against his bare chest.

He looked through the peephole.

"Isabel. Good morning. Come in."

She said no. "I'm taking the train in."

"Why? The car will be here in twenty minutes."

"I'll see you there."

"Isabel, wait." Koons stepped into the hall, one foot in the doorway. "What's on?"

She shrugged. Her old satchel was slung around her shoulder and across her chest. "I like trains."

"OK..." he replied. "But shouldn't we strategize?"

"I'm all set," she said as she tapped the bag and turned on her purple Chuck Taylors.

Sure, of course he felt the chill. But he attributed it to last night. He'd read her wrong. She wanted to party along, to enjoy the night ride. He asked himself if he should hop the train with her. But no. Not the right move for a man about to close a $50 million deal in his own name. As he slipped into his jacket, he laughed at the thought of starting the day on an overcrowded train out of Newark hurdling through a rat-infested tunnel and ending it with Sir Bernie sending his white stretch limo to LAX, the backseat festooned with violets and calla lilies.

Now, though, as the Latina secretary led them along the corridor to the office of Francis Cherry, Koons seesawed between anger and dread. Until last week, though he knew Isabel and her father had walked away from the Federal Witness Protection program, he hadn't known she was in fact Shara Bliss, daughter of a murder victim. Nor did he know the victim was the daughter of Seymour Riegel, a powerful partner in a law firm atop any list of New York's most respected and feared.

Koons knew the firm didn't have an entertainment division; if it had, it would've been a significant presence in LA. So when Isabel introduced her grandfather to him in Cerasus's lobby, Koons was perplexed. Then offended: Isabel wanted her own counsel.

Reeling, Koons hadn't yet come to understand what he'd done wrong. He hadn't yet begun to justify his behavior by asking himself if he were the only agent to fail to balance his ambition with the interest of his client.

With a curious underhand blow, Negron knocked once on Mr. Cherry's door, hitting a dead spot.

Then she pushed it open.

Cherry came around his desk to greet Isabel. He was drinking a Jamba Juice smoothie through a straw.

"You must love these things, right? You being in Cali and all that." He pointed to the sofa. "Sit with me."

A little turtle was plodding its way across financial magazines on the coffee table.

Cherry pointed. "You I know."

"No, I don't believe we've met," Seymour Riegel said as he sat in a wing chair near his granddaughter.

"Not at Capote's Black and White Ball? Or was that Averell Harriman?"

Riegel smiled. Capote's party was in '66. Though Cherry's shaved head, taut skin and fit frame made it impossible to divine his age with any accuracy, Riegel thought he might be in his early 40s.

"And you. Michael Koons. The eager agent."

"Good to know you, Mr. Cherry," Koons said as he sat in the leather wing chair to Cherry's left.

"I like your turtle," Isabel said.

"You don't do that to a turtle. Paint the Twin Towers on its back," Cherry said. He wore Donald Duck braces and slacks from a Brioni suit that cost $43,000. "I opened an account at Schwab in its name. TT Turtle now owns one percent of a media company in Denmark."

"Egmont?" Koons said.

Over a slurping sound from the straw and cup, Cherry said, "I shouldn't reveal. Don't you agree, Mr. Riegel?"

Riegel tilted his head just so.

"All right. So where are we? Oh wait," Cherry said. He sprang from the sofa: to his desk, on the intercom, back to the sofa.

The turtle moved an inch.

A very tall Korean man entered after a single knock on the door.

"Take my seat," Cherry said, pointing.

The Korean man walked to the desk and sat in Cherry's high-back chair.

"You remember Koo," Cherry said to Koons.

Isabel looked at her grandfather.

Eyes at half-mast, Koo didn't move.

To Riegel, Cherry said, "Koo's the one you have to convince."

Koons shifted his briefcase to his lap and popped the clasps. "I have here a copy of the financial projections—"

Cherry said, "Stop. The picture's not going to make any money the way you've got it structured now. Am I right, Koo?"

From over there, Koo said, "You are right, Mr. Cherry."

"But that's OK. I know how you guys work." Cherry shifted on the sofa. "Isabel, all this, numbers and the rest: It's good for you?"

"Not really, no."

"'Not really, no,'" said Francis Cherry. "Well now…"

Koons said, "Mr. Cherry, my client isn't conversant in these matters. We tend to leave these things to—"

"She looks conversant to me."

"Of course. That isn't a criticism. Let me begin again. I—"

"Sy?"

Koo had compiled a dossier on Mr. Riegel, grandfather to Shara Bliss alias Isabel Jellico and father to the late Moira Riegel Bliss. At the mention of the name Bliss, Cherry had pulsed with the thrill of proximity.

"In brief, Blabberdashery, as it is presently constituted, is disadvantageous to my client," Riegel said. "Were you committed to fund all or part of the project, we would propose a new arrangement between yourself and my granddaughter."

Koons's briefcase began to slide off his lap.

"Koo?" said Cherry.

"As a limited liability partnership, Blabberdashery ceases to exist if any principal partner withdraws."

Turning to Koons, Cherry said, "With Riyadh gone—"

"Jenga," said Isabel Jellico.

"Hey, I get that," Cherry said. "The little wooden things. All fall down."

Panicking, Koons said, "Warren Judy—"

Cherry said, "The producer. I hear he's got a track record. You want him on Team Isabel?"

Riegel said, "That's premature—"

"Let the kid talk, Sy," Cherry said. "She can see the finish line."

"I think we leave all options on the table," she replied.

Cherry smiled. "You writers are something. You know how to make it sound like you know what you're doing."

She said, "I wrote the book. The option reverts to me. I know that."

"Isabel," said Koons, wrestling panic. "I'm not sure you understand—"

Cherry said, "I wouldn't go that route, Koons. She understands."

Francis Cherry stood. Then he turned, dropped a knee on the sofa and looked down to the hustle-bustle on Broad Street. A new week. Who among the huddled masses would fleece? Who would be fleeced? You never can tell. Yes you can. That mix of desperation and greed has its own stench. Sniff. Yep, there it is, rising from Koons. A weak play with the kid. What did he have going besides her? Oh wait. Yes. That.

As he turned to sit, Cherry asked, "Sy, you have something in writing?"

"We can have something to you by four."

"Send it to Koo."

Koo snapped at the sound of his name. For a moment, he was reliving the marriage-recommitment ceremony on Xophylia Prime. Gx was radiant, her marigold skin sparkling in the square moon's glow.

"Koo," Cherry said, "worm it through Legal, but tell them it works. I want it finalized by Friday, an eighth of a second before the closing bell rings."

Isabel Jellico stood.

Cherry shook her hand. "I'm going to read your book someday."

"It makes an excellent gift," she said. "Buy in bulk."

Cherry reached to Riegel. "Say hello to Max," he said, referencing the founder and senior partner of Riegel's firm. "Tell him I said 'Shoshanna's brisket.' He'll know what you mean."

Ashen, Koons tried to stand.

"You," Cherry said. "Stay."

With a snap of his head, he told Koo to escort the writer and her lawyer grandfather to the elevator.

In the elevator, she said something.

Riegel said, "Excuse me…"

"Look." She held out her hand. "I'm shaking."

"You did very well, Shara."

"I joke when I'm nervous. Mom did that."

I know…

"He was right, though," she said. "He knew I was pretending."

"He was too," Riegel said as the elevator reached the ground floor. "No one understands Francis Cherry."

They stepped through a waiting crowd to enter the lobby. "But we're getting what we came for, no?"

Riegel nodded. But he was intrigued. Cherry didn't want to be in the motion-picture business. If he did, there were easier ways for him to buy in.

They stepped onto Broad Street. It was chilly in the morning shadows.

"What about Michael?"

Focus your anger, Riegel was tempted to say. It's a useful ally. "Did he tell you he met with Koo? That he shared the data?"

She shook her head.

"You might consider it a lesson learned for Mr. Koons. One day he may realize your response was appropriate."

Riegel then advised her to avoid contact with her former agent until the new contract was signed and a production company was formed. She nodded. He could tell she was already gone.

"Can I try to convince you to stay?" he asked. "Your grandmother would love it."

She shifted her satchel to squeeze his hand. She smiled.

"Take the car," he said, gesturing toward his driver.

Backpedaling, she said, "I'm good, Zeyde."

He watched as she disappeared, wading through the plodding crowd that rose from the subway.

Ian Goldsworthy was across the street, tucked next to Federal Hall, the tall, silver-haired ex-spy puffy and absent stealth, his suit a riot of wrinkles. Over by the old Morgan Bank, a soldier posed for photos with children, the nozzle of his M4 Carbine pointed to cobblestone.

Surely luck had abandoned Goldsworthy. And yet…

She favored her father: the shape of the face, many of the features; Goldsworthy remembered Bliss was tall. So was she. The easy stride. She had that too.

Or did she? Goldsworthy had no reason to trust his judgment. No thought was verifiable. He'd been fully unraveled, every thread pulled. He was undone.

And yet…

Blinking, coughing into his fist, he marshaled his concentration, crossed Broad Street and, strolling along a police barricade, entered the lobby of the building where Cerasus kept its offices and where he was once employed. The security staff knew him; they may have been aware that his clearance had been revoked. But he was recognizable, and all he asked for was a moment with the sign-in sheet.

Seymour Riegel.

Shara Bliss/Isabel Jellico.

Goldsworthy exited. Wavering steps carried him against the human flow toward the Wall Street underground station.

The girl stood at the center of the long underground platform. She waited for the uptown express.

From a distance, Goldsworthy watched as she rummaged around her bag, found a crumpled tissue, dabbed at tears.

The express train arrived with sparks and a squeal.

As he sat, Cherry moved the turtle back to where it began its trek, though not before placing a sliver of lettuce an inch or so away from its head.

Dazed, Koons watched.

"How did you let that happen, Koons? You were outplayed by a college kid."

He replied weakly. "Isabel is no ordinary college kid."

"I hope not. I'm about to give her fifty million dollars."

Koons had yet to recover. No element of his fantasy remained. All he had envisioned was gone. "I don't believe this arrangement is in your best—"

"Yes it is."

"But in effect you're partnering with—"

"I suppose you know why you're here," Cherry said, drawing up.

Fully resigned, Koons replied. "I have no idea."

"Make the call."

Cherry's gaze locked Koons in place.

"Make the call," he repeated.

"Mr. Cherry—"

"Call her father. Call Donnie Bliss now."

Though utterly confused, Koons stretched out a leg to dip for his phone.

Cherry inched to the sofa's edge as Koons scrolled for the number. "Give," he said when Koons stopped.

Cherry pressed the key with his thumb.

18

Bliss woke slowly. Confused, he tapped at the carpet until he found his phone. He recognized the calling number.

Expecting Koons, he said, "Michael."

"Donald Harry Bliss. Francis Cherry."

Francis Cherry. New York. Francis Cherry, who hired the man who had beaten him senseless. Cherry sent hit men to retrieve stolen goods.

His back stiff from sleeping on the floor, he placed his hand on the carpeting to stand. "How did you—"

"You mean besides Koons giving you up?"

Bliss walked toward the window.

"You're in Memphis." Cherry then said the name of the hotel.

Bliss threw back the curtains. Bright sunlight burst into the room. Shading his eyes, he said, "Let me talk to Michael."

Koons was looking nowhere. He was biting the skin on his thumb.

Cherry said, "He's indisposed. Look, Donnie, here's the situation: I just gave your daughter fifty million dollars."

"You—"

"By the way, she's a beauty. I mean, under the hoodie and the wacky outfit and the hair and all that."

"You're in Los Angeles?"

"Negative."

"Then how—"

"She came with your father-in-law."

"She's in New York?"

"I bought the movie, Donnie. And I bought you."

Heart racing, Bliss turned his back to the window. "I don't—"

"You work for me." Cherry kicked off his shoes and stretched out on the sofa. "Full benefits, dental, eye care, four weeks vacation, a company car. Generous expense account and you're vested in the pension plan from day one."

Pacing, Bliss said, "Is she all right?"

"Your kid? She's super. No, you don't have to worry about her. She's golden."

She's all right. Sy was with her. Francis Cherry. Fifty million dollars. Financing. Bliss was beginning to understand.

Cherry ran his hand along his shaved head. "As for Mr. Koons here, he's not all right."

Bliss said, "Is it in the contract?"

"If by 'it' you mean 'you,' I'll say this about that: Do you want her to know?"

Bliss looked down to the street below. Tourists had yet to descend.

"Or maybe you do. Dad rides to the rescue. Would that play?"

"No," Bliss said.

"Fine. It's our secret. If Koons here squeals, kill him any way you like."

Standing again, Bliss said, "Where is she?"

"They're gone. If you'd like, I can have her followed."

"Don't," Bliss said.

"Want me to monitor the airlines?"

Bliss wondered if Riegel would take his call.

"Hey, Donnie. Sorry about that billboard stunt. Not really. But, you know, that's me. What the fuck, right?"

Fifty million dollars. Sy protects Pup. The film gets made.

"We square?" Cherry asked as he wriggled to his feet.

"Maybe so," Bliss said.

"Great. When can you report?"

Ginger Stillwell went looking for Biloxi Box, Donnie Bliss saying it was a landmark by the river near where the woman lived, the one named Lola who'd been in the pickup with the man who chased her out of town. No one could tell her that man didn't have something to do with Boone's death. Seeing as he came after Bliss and her as soon as he saw their photo on the Web, that innocent, it-means-nothing photo, it stood to reason he was a man of violent action and that meant he killed Boone. For the reward. She was going to prove it. It was her responsibility, given the damned cops weren't about to do their jobs.

Actually, she knew for a fact it wasn't her responsibility. But even just driving toward Biloxi Box made her feel better than she had when she was driving away.

She located the redbrick factory, the lettering on the façade faded. Diamond gates covered the windows that were tinted by age. Hard neighborhood: broken gutters on the houses, holes in the screen doors.

Up one block, down the next, as she looked for a red pickup, the kind she saw swerve and squeal to a stop at the record studio. Speckled sunlight, but nothing, even after a half hour. Then a full 60 minutes.

She needed a clever way to get someone to give up the address.

She drove over to Sun Studio, Boone's car rattling, the needle dipping toward E.

Tour buses out front. Had that Lola seen her with Bliss?

Of course she had.

She slept with him, and there he was with another woman, right outside where she works, standing right by his side. How do you think she's going to take that?

Ginger didn't believe she could pull it off: a phone call to the studio's office; a ruse to get her running, something about a flash fire or a break-in; can you confirm your address?

Damn it. I'm not equipped, she thought as she drove on. I'm not going to get outside myself.

She groped for her cell phone, one eye on the road.

She eased the car under knotty branches of a shade tree.

"Hey, Cotillion," she said.

"Ginger, where are you?"

"I'm in Memphis. Where are you?"

Cotillion said, "I'm at school."

"In class? Oh damn. I'm sorry—"

"I'm crossing the parking lot. Ginger, are you on the road?"

Cutting the engine, she said, "I need you to do me a favor."

"Are you OK? You sound all agitated."

"One quick favor."

"What did he do?"

"Cotillion—"

"I figured as much: He stuck around to play with you. Didn't he?"

"No he did not," she said. "Listen, I need you to make a call for me. Will you?"

Cotillion put her books on a bench. "You'll come home then?"

"Cotillion..."

Soon, Ginger Stillwell was parked across from Sun Studio. Either that Lola woman was going to come out running and hop in her car, or that thug she was with was going to rip around the corner and—

The red pickup skidded to a halt behind a big tour bus with Korean lettering on its flank.

The thug leaned on the horn.

The bus driver looked out his side window.

Lola appeared, worried, hurrying.

A call about a gas leak got them going.

Thank you, Cotillion.

Ginger implored Boone's car to run on fumes while she followed.

Hot water cascading down his back, steam filling the room, Donnie Bliss could not discern what his next move might be.

Go to Los Angeles, see Koons and find out what happened.

Head east to meet with Cherry.

New York was out. He wasn't going there. Not as Donnie Bliss, Sam Jellico, John Bleak, J.J. Walk, Frank Niewidzialny. Not as anybody.

Cherry knew that before he made the deal. They' d spoken once; still recovering from the beating, Bliss told him: I'm not going to New York.

Cherry tricked Pup into returning to the city where her mother was murdered and everything spun down to a deep hell.

But no, Pup was too cautious to be duped by a stranger. It was Michael. He convinced her. He sold out Pup for the funding. Pup asked Sy for help—smart; good for you, Pup—and Sy used Koons's misstep to broker a new deal.

Moira wouldn't tolerate betrayal either. Though Moira couldn't live with anger. Pup could. She did. Pup didn't sulk, at least not for long. Pup acted. She could turn her heart to stone.

Bliss rinsed the shampoo from his hair.

He remembered he intended to buy six new shirts today.

What did Cherry want him to do?

Cherry thought he' d killed the man in Los Angeles.

He said, "If Koons squeals, kill him any way you like."

Security? Personal protection?

Bliss thought back to his meeting with Cherry. In a restaurant in Newark. Cherry had a man with him. Tall, silver-haired; obvious: He leaned out of the restaurant booth. Bliss could feel his gaze when he sat with his back to him. The silver-haired man—British?—studied Bliss as he exited.

If Cherry already has security, what's the job?

How much did Cherry know about Donald Harry Bliss, son of Mendocino County, man without a home?

Bliss asked himself what he knew about Francis Cherry.

Cherry had a taste for revenge.

Billboard Man, you are my instrument of revenge.

Revenge, thought Donnie Bliss as he reached for the faucet.

To Goldsworthy's surprise, Isabel Jellico didn't hop a flight out of Newark back to LAX. Instead she headed to Northern California. Oakland International.

Goldsworthy decided to follow. He was on the same flight. Isabel Jellico took the window seat in the last row in coach. Hoodie up, strings tight, she slept with her head against the plastic shade. More than once, Goldsworthy walked to the back of the plane to check on her.

She was dear to Billboard Man, and now she was dear to Cherry.

Goldsworthy knew Cherry had hired her to write his life story. The Rise and Rise of Francis Cherry.

All honor and glory to her if she can determine who he is under that façade: Francis Cherry, a figment of his own imagination, a man who spun himself from magic cloth.

Goldsworthy stood in the aisle as the plane cleared the Great Lakes. Looking back toward the last row, he saw leverage curled in a deep sleep.

Gassing up Boone's car, Ginger realized she needed to organize. Clean up, eat, charge her cell phone. Think a little bit. Finalize a plan.

She asked for the restroom key, but the attendant told her the toilet was out of order and, lady, you don't want to go in there anyway.

Pork rinds and a grape Slurpee wouldn't get it done, no.

Maybe they'll let her plug in her phone at a fast-food place.

I know where they live. Now what am I supposed to do?

She opened her purse to put away the change and there it was: the key to Room 632.

Back in the car, the tank full.

Bliss had advised in favor of caution, so she parked a ways over on the street by the ball field, people going here and there.

She turned a corner. Up ahead, a Dumpster was filled with old wooden flooring torn from a nearby brick building. Beyond it, she saw the awning above the hotel's side entrance.

She wondered if Donnie was still in the hotel. She could use his room. It might be dangerous to go back to 632. Caution.

I'll explain why I returned. He won't agree, but I'll explain.

Charge the phone, freshen up, make it snappy.

God, didn't a cup of coffee sound good right about now?

Head down, she dug into her bag to retrieve the key to open the side entrance.

Joe Blunt charged from behind the Dumpster, raised his fist and punched Ginger Stillwell in the back of the head. She was unconscious before she hit the sidewalk.

The Ford pickup skidded to a stop, Lola Styles behind the wheel.

"Let's go," Joe Blunt said with a wave.

Memories of the selfsame blow to her own head rekindled, Lola Styles hopped down and hurried around the flatbed. Without thinking, she reached up and stroked where she'd been hit.

Joe Blunt whipped off his belt. He tossed it to her.

"Tie her ankles," he said as he opened her bag. "Double quick."

She slid to her knees.

Lifting her wallet, Joe Blunt read her driver's license. "Yeah," he said, "it's Stillwell's wife."

Lola Styles tightened the belt. Ginger, the woman Boone was so eager to impress. And she's still here in Memphis. She's trying to work us into owning up.

Wonder what that kind of two-way devotion is like.

"Lola, goddamn it," Joe Blunt barked. "Stop your daydream and get to it."

"I'm on it, Joe. Jesus."

He was pocketing the Stillwell girl's money.

She was out and drooling so Joe Blunt dumped her in the truck bed and he told Lola Styles to scoot over and they roared away and drove back to their place, the new motherfuckin' clutch sensor working all right and don't think for a minute he's not going to feel it for that little stunt, Donald Harry Bliss, Mr. Billboard Man.

Joe Blunt carried her over his shoulder. He tossed her on the sofa. She bounced on the Titan blue-and-white crocheted throw.

"Wake her up," he said as he took off his nylon jacket.

Over by the door, Lola Styles blew on her cold hands. She stepped up.

Joe Blunt was breathing hard, his throat dry from the work. Over by the laptop and his knitting needles, there was a half-empty beer bottle on the table.

"I think her nose is broken, Joe. The way she hit the door."

Now Joe Blunt rooted through her bag for her cell. He said, "Wake her up."

She untied Ginger Stillwell's ankles and wrists.

Her brains scrambled, that girl wasn't going nowhere.

She tapped Ginger's cheek.

Joe Blunt left the living room, boot heels thudding.

"Ginger," whispered Lola Styles.

Tapped her cheeks again.

Her head lolled. Blood collected at her nostrils.

"Come on, you," Lola Styles said.

Joe Blunt returned. He flung a measuring cup of cold water into the girl's face. He tossed the cup aside. He grabbed a fistful of hair.

Ginger Stillwell blinked, sputtered.

Joe Blunt used that fistful of hair to get her to her feet.

Lola Styles cupped her under the arms.

"Nose ain't broken," said Joe Blunt. "She's got no complaints."

Ginger Stillwell moaned. She shook her head.

19

Using the passing crowd for cover, Ian Goldsworthy was waiting in the terminal, hanging at the waterspout by the newsstand until Isabel Jellico passed.

Outside in the overcast Oakland afternoon, a stout, dark-skinned man in a straw cowboy hat was waiting too, his dusty boot heel on the running board of an old baby-blue-and-white Willys Jeep station wagon caked with mud. Wipers had pushed the dirt to the sides of the windshield.

The man smiled as Isabel appeared, not too much though. He reached for her bag, but she hugged him and the Mexican man seemed surprised. Then he relented, patting her on the head. Goldsworthy couldn't hear what they were saying.

On the side of the Jeep, in faded gold letters, HORACE JONES, MENDOCINO, USA.

"Paco," Isabel said as she opened her arms. Morales looked tired, weathered, gaunt. A pearl button was loose on his shirt, which had been bleached white by the sun. She knew he worked the ranch until he dropped; her grandfather couldn't do it like he used to. "¿*Como andas*?" she said cheerfully.

Morales was reserved by nature. He'd known Shara for as long as he could remember, but he never addressed her with what he felt was an inappropriate level of warmth.

She hugged him.

"OK, Shara," he said, his accent thick.

"How is Tatyana?" Somehow, Morales had married a Russian woman, plump and jovial.

"Oh, you know."

"I do," Shara said. "And Alex? Out of Kuwait, I heard."

"In Germany. Thank God."

"And my grandfather?"

Now Paco Morales smiled. "A grouchy old pain in the tail."

Shara Bliss laughed. "Not much has changed, has it?"

The passenger's side door opened with a groan.

"Don't let her sit," Joe Blunt said as he returned. "Make her—Jesus. You are a stupid bitch."

Lola Styles retreated.

Ginger Stillwell looked at the sawed-off shotgun Joe Blunt had at his side.

With a free hand, he grabbed her chin and squeezed.

"You're fine. You hear me? You're fine and now you're going to do what you're told."

She opened her eyes wide. She nodded.

"I'm letting go of you now," Joe Blunt said. "You scream, you run, and I put a big hole in you."

Ginger stood tall. Though the center of her face and the back of her head throbbed and ached, her senses had returned. She decided to shut up and listen and do whatever the scowling man said.

"Where is he?"

"I don't know," she said.

He raised the shotgun and held it shoulder high, the stock aimed at her face.

"I honestly don't."

"Joe..."

"Don't make me...I swear to God, I will crack you broke open."

"Joe," Lola Styles said, "let her tell it."

Ginger turned. "I don't know the man."

"Bullshit." Joe Blunt said that.

"I met him, we had a time, all of a sudden he showed up here when I had to retrieve...my husband's body."

Lola looked at Joe Blunt, who was shaking his head.

He said, "No. It don't add up."

"Well, it does if you consider the newspapers were saying he killed Boone," Ginger said.

"Get him back."

"I don't know why he would come."

Joe Blunt took her phone from his pocket.

He looked at the tiny screen.

Ginger Stillwell and Lola Styles exchanged a glance.

Joe Blunt lifted the phone to his ear.

Bliss was on I-55, heading north, Carbondale more or less a straight shot, three and a half hours off. He'd already passed Marion. He was thinking maybe it was going to rain, and then his phone rang.

Pup, he thought.

Or Francis Cherry.

He didn't recognize the number.

He kept an eye on the road.

"I'm going to blow her face right off her head if you don't get over here right this minute."

"Biloxi Box," said Donnie Bliss. "Clutch sensor."

"You call the cops, she's dead."

"Who?" Bliss said, though he knew full well it was Ginger Stillwell.

"Don't fuck with me, Billboard Man."

He tapped the blinker and shifted into the right lane. "What's the plan?" he asked.

"Gather everything you own."

He said, "Everything I own is on my back."

"Well then we got us a problem."

Horace Jones Bed and Breakfast was one thing, the ranch another. A glossy pamphlet in the lobby of a rest stop told him all about the business: Northern California cuisine, wine from Napa and Sonoma, massage therapy, Wi-Fi in the lodge, bird-watching, yoga, horseback riding. Tour a working ranch. Horses and cattle. Horace Jones came west in 1865. He fought off wolves and grizzlies to raise horses. He surveyed the land and bought wisely. Today, the memory of Horace Jones and the settlers of Mendocino County lives on in rustic splendor as…

Paying cash, Goldsworthy acquired a hunting rifle, ammo and binoculars outside Geyserville. A Winchester Model 70. He didn't know if he could shoot it with any accuracy—the assault rifles MI6 handed out required little skill to operate—but he had to go with what he could get. A handgun would require reams of paperwork and proper identification, which meant waiting time and soon a red flag waved before the eyes of the CIA.

The B&B was on a grassy hilltop, a cedar castle with bay windows surrounded by stout bushes and, in the distance, imposing redwoods that seemed to quiver in the gathering moonlight. A paved road led to the hotel. Two Land Rovers were sentries in the scoop. Off to the side of the main property sat a pond for canoeing. On a veranda, a group of men in business-casual wear drank beer from longnecks around a crackling fire.

Goldsworthy finished off a Bombay gin mini. Then another.

The ranch was about a mile down the road, maybe two, rushing rapids cleaving the expanse. It was hidden beneath the rolling hills. Goldsworthy drove his rented 4X4 to a bend. The ranch was below, secure with only one wide bumpy path to enter and exit. In the vast adjacent field, cows nibbled at bales of hay.

He parked the vehicle. He crossed the dirt road and, his free hand in the turf for balance, climbed until he found a nesting spot.

The break in the tree trunk was a tad high, but it was suitable. He snuggled the rifle's forestock into the break. He looked through the sight.

The dusty blue-and-white Jeep was parked on gravel near a side door. Lights were on inside. Goldsworthy thought he might be facing a kitchen, gingham curtains tied back. He put down the rifle and stepped away from the tree.

With the binoculars, he had a wider view. Tighter too. The kitchen, yes. A plump woman hurried past the window. Was she singing to herself? To someone? The sink was under the window. Now she worked.

There were lights on upstairs too.

Bliss left his blazer in the car, folded neatly in the backseat. He'd untucked his oxford, revealing its wrinkled tails.

He came up the steps, the rental's tire iron slid down in his jeans. Maybe he would need it, maybe not. He'd seen men like this one before. Dangerous, but dim-witted. The man wasn't thinking about anything but the payoff. It was a stupid play, arrogant. If he didn't kill Boone Stillwell, Lola's man was doing all he could to make it look like he did.

Coming out of the bedroom, Lola Styles opened the front door.

Bliss nodded.

Joe Blunt was seated. Ginger stood next to him.

Joe Blunt had the shotgun barrel hard under her chin.

"Billboard Man," he said.

Bliss showed Joe Blunt his empty hands. "Let her go and whatever you want is yours," he said.

"Give me what I want and I let her go," Joe Blunt replied.

Lola Styles closed the door. She leaned against it. She was directly behind Bliss and she saw the head of the metal rod pressing against his shirt.

Joe Blunt said, "Otherwise, I will kill her. Don't make a damned bit of difference to me."

Ginger Stillwell trembled in terror. Tears glistened on her cheeks.

Bliss looked at the blood crusted to her nose. "You had to hit her, didn't you?"

"I did indeed."

"Says here you won't hit me," Bliss went on.

"Don't," Lola Styles whispered.

"Listen to her, Billboard Man. Listen to your coochie."

Bliss circled to his left, moving toward the TV. His palms remained open.

"Throw down your wallet," Joe Blunt said.

"I don't carry my money in my wallet. I've got a couple of thousand dollars in my shoe."

Bliss used the heel of one sneaker on the heel of the other and it slipped free. He flipped it toward Lola Styles.

She dug out the bills. She held them up for Joe Blunt to see.

"That's a start," he said.

Eyes on Joe Blunt, Bliss stepped out of his other shoe. He wanted balance when the attack came. "Now let her go," he said.

Lola Styles said, "It's twenty-three hundred dollars, Joe."

Joe Blunt looked at his girl. "From a man who's got millions."

Bliss laughed. "You are way misinformed."

"Oh, is that right, Mr. Donald Harry Bliss? You're saying your wife wasn't daughter to a shitload of money?"

"That's her family's money, Joe."

"And it's not your family no more?"

As Joe Blunt inched forward on the sofa, Ginger Stillwell felt the shotgun ease under her chin.

"You're telling me they won't pay up to dig you out of a hole?"

Bliss said, "I had you for half a moron last night, but you're the full dose, aren't you?"

"We'll see who's smart and who ain't soon enough, Billboard Man."

Bliss had himself set now.

He looked at Ginger. He looked at Joe Blunt. He put his hands in his back pockets.

"No," he said. "I'm thinking about you and those star tattoos. They tell me something."

Joe Blunt kept his eyes fixed hard on Bliss.

Leaning in, Bliss said, "They tell me you don't know how to come at a man."

Joe Blunt sneered. "You think I'm gonna fall for that shit—"

Ginger Stillwell fell back as Bliss swung the tire iron. It hit the shotgun, knocking it to the floor, and now Bliss was on Joe Blunt. He raised the tire iron again and he brought it down. Joe Blunt dodged the blow, wriggled free and jumped to his feet. He grabbed Bliss's arm before he could swing it again.

Bliss strained to shake his arm free. As they struggled, Joe Blunt's heel hit the shotgun, spinning it under the sofa.

Bliss bumped up against the coffee table, and then he fell back, Joe Blunt on top. The table shattered.

Bliss held on to the tire iron, but Joe Blunt had his arm. The two men grunted and trembled.

Ginger retreated, stumbling to the kitchen. She saw a beer bottle and knitting needles, meager weapons if Joe Blunt snapped the tire iron from Bliss's hand.

Now Bliss was on top again, and he managed to slip free and get his knees under him. He set to bring down the tire iron.

Joe Blunt kicked with two feet and sent Bliss tumbling back.

Scrambling, Joe Blunt groped under the sofa for the shotgun.

Before Bliss could recover to strike again, Joe Blunt had it.

From his knees, he pointed it at Bliss.

"Now who's the—"

A shot rang out. Bliss couldn't help but recoil.

When Bliss opened his eyes, Joe Blunt was bleeding through a hole in the side of his head, a look of stunned confusion in his eyes.

Bliss turned.

Lola Styles was holding a pearl-handle pistol.

Ginger said, "Ol' Buddy."

Legs wide, Lola Styles pointed Boone Stillwell's gun at Bliss.

"Lola," he said as he stood. He let the tire iron fall.

Knitting needle in her hand, Ginger tiny-stepped toward Bliss just as Joe Blunt collapsed.

He hit the floor with a dull thud, blood spurting.

Now Lola Styles walked toward Bliss. Then she passed him.

"Lola," Bliss said again.

She pumped another round into Joe Blunt's head. And then another.

"Get out of here," she said to Bliss. "Both of you. Go now."

Then she sat herself on the sofa, Ol' Buddy dangling from her fingers.

Ian Goldsworthy threw back the last of the Bombay gin minis and returned to his post. Stars were scattered overhead; he could smell the pines. He shivered in the cool night air. It was difficult to see. Light from the kitchen window spread across the gravel. The old Jeep hadn't moved.

The moment Isabel Jellico stepped outside, the minute she opened the bedroom window, Goldsworthy would have his revenge against Cherry, against Donald Harry Bliss, and he would return to New York as the victor, a proven man, a man necessary to the security of Francis Cherry's future.

If Cherry didn't bring him back into Cerasus, all Wall Street would know he'd been sent to kill the daughter of the man on the billboard, the man who would not accept Cherry's advances. Wall Street, all of New York, everyone in America would know Cherry wanted to break the man who said no to him.

Goldsworthy steadied the rifle in the breech.

He rubbed and dug his heels into the turf.

He waited.

The door opened.

Goldsworthy flexed his trigger finger.

At the door, draped in shadows, a hoodie appeared.

Goldsworthy squeezed off a round.

The bullet struck the hoodie.

Goldsworthy stared in amazement. Good God. The shot. The shot struck the—

"You."

Goldsworthy turned.

From 10 feet away, old Harry Bliss fired a single shot from his Remington rifle, taking off half of Ian Goldsworthy's face at the jaw hinge.

Goldsworthy slammed against the tree and slid to the ground. He gurgled as he tried to speak.

Harry Bliss stepped up and shoved the butt end of the rifle stock against Goldsworthy's neck. The gray-haired rancher under the tattered ball cap leaned his full weight on the dying man's throat.

Down below at the ranch, Paco Morales examined Isabel's hoodie, the one he extended with the working end of a broomstick.

As he leaned away from the dead man's body, old grizzled Harry Bliss rubbed his salt-and-pepper beard and took the flashlight out of his back pocket. He turned it on and waved it so Morales could see he was all right.

Isabel walked to Morales's side. He dropped his arm on her shoulder.

Up on the hill, Harry Bliss looked at the body. He turned the head with the toe of his boot.

"Who the hell are you?"

He kneeled to dig out the dead man's wallet.

He used his own phone to call the sheriff.

First thing Harry Bliss said when he reached his granddaughter at the house: "It's not him."

20

I have no idea," said Donnie Bliss.

Ginger Stillwell asked him what he thought would happen to Lola Styles.

There they were again. Outside the police station in Memphis.

He said, "She put herself at risk. She saved our lives."

"Her Joe killed Boone and she knew."

At least, thought Donnie Bliss.

After a while, Ginger Stillwell said, "Ol' Buddy, huh?"

"Ol' Buddy."

Sipp and Milton had arrived at the dead man's apartment after the uniforms did, but not in time to stop Lola Styles from putting three in her tormentor. Bliss had called the cops as he headed toward the old Biloxi Box factory. Counting the minutes while he taunted Joe Blunt, he' d begun to think Sipp and Milton were strolling to the rescue, Sipp styling his hair, Milton sucking on some pork ribs.

Outside the building, as the EMT crew examined Ginger's wounds, he told the cops he didn't know what to make of Lola Styles. But he figured the star tattoos said something about her plight.

He said, "That man was going to kill her too."

Tugging on his tie, Sipp replied, "Probably."

At the station, they gave Bliss his $2,300. But they kept Ol' Buddy as evidence.

Pacing the street, Bliss made a couple of phone calls and then waited for Ginger Stillwell. Shivering, he turned up his blazer collar. He was thinking it was almost time for a winter coat. There was a brand he preferred.

He spent most of last winter in Texas: Laredo, Alice, Corpus Christi. He slept away Christmas Eve in San Antonio.

Maybe Miami, Florida, this year. Miami, where he would hardly need a coat.

He'd tell Francis Cherry he was going to Miami.

But he was going to Carbondale first. He intended to turn back the clock, to see if he could wash away Billboard Man and Donnie Bliss too.

Now Ginger Stillwell said, "So...that's it."

Bliss walked to the rental car. He opened the door for her. "That's it."

They already debated the cost of shipping Boone's wreck back to Jerome. It was less than you'd think.

He drove her to Memphis International. He pulled up and parked out front and got out like it was any old building. If they towed the car, that was fine. He knew how to get to Carbondale via St. Louis.

"It says Arrivals," Ginger told him as he popped the trunk to retrieve her bags.

They walked through the exiting crowd. People shuffled, fatigued from travel.

Someone had turned the heat on in the vestibule.

He waited for her to pass.

A National Guardsman with a German shepherd stood over there.

Ginger stopped. Bliss put down her bags.

In jeans and an old suede coat, Cotillion was walking right at them, her long black hair flowing, her gait steady and determined.

Ginger scurried toward her. They hugged hard and tight, rocking.

"Oh, Cotillion. You don't know."

"It's all right, Ginger. It's over now."

"I do need to go home," she said through tears.

"We're going," Cotillion said.

Ginger stepped back. "How did you—Did he—"

"He did. The ticket was waiting. Plus two to go home too."

Ginger Stillwell turned to thank Donnie Bliss.

But he was already gone.

The Mendocino County sheriff's department had men up on the hill and another car, lights whirling, engine purring, outside the ranch house. Irascible old Harry Bliss, he finally went and did it. He shot somebody with that damned Remington. Shot a man square in the face, dropped him dead.

Tatyana Morales tried to drape a blanket on the old man's shoulders and he threw her a look like she was next on the firing line.

Up on the hill, they yellow-taped the area to keep out all those gawking, light-beer-drinking middle managers from Sacramento who were getting more than they bargained for on their team-building retreat. The proprietors wanted everyone gone quickly, as in right now, seeing as a man having his face blown off might stir the spirits up at the B&B, disputing the notion that the air, the redwoods, the rushing rapids, the in-room crystals were a tonic for all that ails, save death by rifle fire.

The sheriff's men assured them it was cut-and-dried: Eighty-two-year-old Harry was defending his granddaughter and Paco and Tat, the livestock, and your property too, come to think of it. From who? That drunken Brit. Address back east. We're working it ass-end to front now. What they call reverse engineering.

Below at the ranch house, a deputy had all she was going to get out of Harry Bliss.

Harry said:

"Man came. Man's gone.

"Point a rifle at me and mine? No, I don't think he'll be doing that twice.

"No. No indeed. Man shot before I could call him.

"Of course he turned. How the hell you think I shot his face? I came up hard. Goddamn it, Lorraine. What, I was supposed to excuse myself before I interrupted?

"She's fine. Ain't no peckerhead gonna scare Shara off. She's mine to the marrow, ain't she?"

At that point, Tatyana stepped up. She dropped her hand on Harry's bony arm. She said, her accent a peculiar mix of Russian and English via Mexico, "Maybe you go to your granddaughter now, *Abuelo*, huh?"

Deputy Lorraine Perez spoke into her shoulder mike. The sheriff said fine. We'll pick it up in the morning.

By then maybe we'll know why the U.S. Marshal's office in Eureka is so damned interested.

They all waited up to see if Harry Bliss was going to crack to show even a sliver of emotion. But he did not. Paco and Tatyana went to bed finally, and so did Shara, who was caught between East Coast and West Coast time. Cup of black coffee in a chipped ceramic mug, Harry stared out the window with his elbows on the long table that predated his tenure at the Horace Jones ranch, long before it was a B&B, long before he married late, long before his wife ran off and his son of a bitch son wouldn't grow up tall and true like his old man wanted, goddamn it.

Shara came down. Floppy pajamas with clownish monkey faces on them and the damned sweat top with the zipper and a hood with a hole in it.

She sat next to him. They faced the darkness beyond the gingham curtain.

He ignored her. What the hell did she want now?

She said, "Tell me the truth."

"I don't lie, girl. You ought to know that by now."

"You know he wouldn't hurt me. Not like that."

Harry Bliss shrugged.

"You knew it wasn't him."

"Didn't matter either way," he said plainly, his gnarled fingers around the steaming cup.

"You hate him that much?"

He turned his head slowly.

He said, "Don't you?"

She waited until dawn and called New York.

"Bobeshi..." she began. She was a child again. But she didn't need comfort. She wanted someone to explain.

"Oh," her grandmother said as she listened to what sounded like a nightmare come to life. "Oh, Shara."

"The man was trying to shoot me," she said. "I mean, who else? Harry?"

Sy had already left for the office. He needed to know. Rude, ill-mannered, obstinate though he may be, more or less a stranger to the Riegels, Harry Bliss needed counsel, if only for Shara's sake. The ranch was her refuge.

As she paced the vestibule of their apartment, Evelyn Riegel stopped to stare at a photo of Moira in Central Park, carefree and in love. Donnie had taken it and then had it framed as an unexpected gift for his future in-laws. He'd tried hard to win over Sy.

"What can we do, Shara?" she asked. "Anything. Don't hesitate."

"Just listen," Shara said softly. I just need someone to listen.

"Shara," she replied. "Call your father. Please. It's time, sweetheart."

There was nothing for him in Carbondale. He'd done it the first time. For the hell of it, he went back to the bar he'd visited on the previous trip. College kids were still playing tabletop shuffleboard; the same football game was on TV. The young waitress came over. He recognized her, but to her he was just another customer.

He said, "What's good?"

"To tell you the truth, mister, not much. We've got fresh-baked ham. It looks all right."

He went with that. On rye.

"Good choice," she said.

"You have potato salad, coleslaw or something like that?"

"Let me do you a favor and say no." She gave her head a little shake, her pretty face twisted in horror.

He reached for the coat tree and lifted the paperback out of his new coat's pocket.

Francis Cherry was in Kingston, Jamaica, already bored shitless with Miss Venezuela but enamored with the jerk chicken he found at a roadside stand. He returned six times: lunch and dinner on three consecutive days. Finally, he made his move: an offer to relocate the woman and her four kids to Brooklyn and seed a restaurant that could serve as prototype for a national chain. Let's call it Marley's and why not? Common name.

"Mrs. Goodenough," he said to the tall woman in a floral apron and matching bandana, "there are two conditions."

He was sitting on a wooden bench, his fingers and cheeks coated in tangy-spicy sauce. He'd already laid out his proposal, astonishing her regulars and the daffy-eyed herd of goats who lazed nearby. So persuasive was Cherry that several men sent their sons to retrieve Mr. Goodenough. "The first condition: You tell your husband over there to stop glaring at me and put away the machete."

Miss Venezuela watched from the backseat of the stretch limousine. Each night, she did that thing he enjoyed, willingly too, but knew she had disappointed Cherry. He no longer mentioned the probability of her own prime-time telenovela to be simulcast to the entire Spanish-speaking world, a billion-dollar budget for advertising alone. To rectify matters, she was half-hoping the seething black man would cleave him in two. Who then would know she was not the personification of perfection as her publicists insisted?

Cherry removed his straw hat to fan his face. "The second condition is…" He stopped. "Ah, you're not going for it, are you?"

Mrs. Goodenough said with a lilt, "Not for a moment, Mr. Francis Cherry."

"Any chance you'll give me the recipe?"

Now he was back in his hotel suite overlooking the white sands of Montego Bay. He lay on his bed, custom-made white slacks, a belt made from okapi skin. A hole in his white silk socks exposed a big toe.

TT Turtle strolled across a copy of *National Geographic* magazine Cherry had been perusing. Miss Venezuela—"Venezuela, right?"—stuck out her tongue at him whenever he looked down at a page.

"I'm going for a swim," she announced.

"Take TT," he said as he reached for the phone. "And put a top on, huh? Those things are a distraction."

A minute later, Cherry was put through.

"Sir Bernie," he said cheerfully. "How's life in Tinseltown?"

"Francis Cherry," the agency head huffed. "I can't imagine why I should speak to you at all."

"Calm yourself," Cherry said as he sat up, careful not to disturb the turtle, who'd been left behind. "Think pleasant thoughts."

"One pleasant thought would be the knowledge, Francis, that you've come to your senses. I mean, why in good heavens—"

"Whoa. You're stuck in Act Two, friend. Is that how you say it? Act Two."

Blinds drawn to block out the sun and the life-affirming majesty of the San Gabriels, Sir Bernie was in his fuzzy white-on-white conference room, a bowl of unwrapped Hershey's Kisses in front of him. Since the fiasco with Michael Koons that put in jeopardy Isabel Jellico's movie franchise, Sir Bernie had added 18 pounds to his already mountainous frame. Thus far, news of the collapse of Blabberdashery hadn't reached the media. But the director and the male lead were planning to move on. A billion-dollar franchise was about to disappear, and he'd be left to face the wrath of Francis Cherry.

"Act Two. Yes," said Sir Bernie.

"Here's the plan: I flipped the property back to the Saudis. They're in and they're staying. You put Blabberdashery back together any way you want. This guy Judy, the director and his pals, you. Any way you want. My cut comes out of Riyadh. They believe, Sir Bernie."

Bernie giggled. "Is this in writing?"

"In writing," Cherry affirmed. He'd already made $11 million on the deal, a pittance to the bin Abdul-Aziz Al-Saud family, but a good day's work for Cherry.

Sir Bernie hoisted himself out of his chair. "What are the conditions, Francis?"

"You protect the girl. She's in as deep as she wants for as long as she wants."

"We can assure you—"

"She retains the rights to her characters."

"Francis—"

"If she's even a little bit put out, the thing falls down. My friend Fahd moves the money to, I don't know, a casino in Giza, Macao, someplace."

"I understand, Francis."

"The thing gets made. No excuses. And none of this direct-to-Hulu shit. Wherever I go, I want to see it on the marquee at every multi-maxi-gigaplex within a million-mile radius."

Sir Bernie's heart was beating, the syrup blood finagle-oozing its way through a maze of plaque. "It should have that kind of broad appeal."

"You know, I read the book. It's pretty damn good."

Sir Bernie didn't know. He'd read neither the book nor the screenplay. "Indeed."

"Finally, the little shit Koons."

"He's in the mailroom. Done and done."

"There's a right way to do the wrong thing to a client. Remember, I know how you operate."

Sir Bernie gulped. He reached for a chocolate. "I thought we were never to speak of it—"

"Who's speaking?" said Francis Cherry.

Sir Bernie said quickly, "Francis, tell me about the spy. The one who was killed up north. The Brit."

"Nut job. Can you believe MI6 dropped that on me?"

"We hear his target was Isabel."

"They tell me if you had walked out of my office that morning, he would've followed you. He snapped. Drugs, misadventure. A bad egg."

Well, thought Sir Bernie, that bio doesn't much conflict with what I'd heard about Ian Goldsworthy from my sources back home.

"Francis, when—"

"Signing off, Bernie," Cherry said as he cut the line.

He passed the phone to the turtle.

"TT," he said, "get Koo. Tell him I need an update on where our Mr. Donnie Harry Bliss is."

St. Louis wasn't much better, though he met a man he needed to see for paper and a credit card in his new name. He rode the light-rail system, but it wasn't helping him disappear. Five weeks had passed since he pulled out of Memphis, and he couldn't put it away. Not so much the scowling man with the bullets in his face, but the real soul of it: the lecture Cotillion gave him. "What do you need from us?"

He took himself to Clayton to peer into the galleries and then he stepped out of the cold for tapas. A redhead at the bar let it be known she was interested, and he thought she might be all right; an e-reader right there next to a glass of golden tequila and she was pressing up against 40, meaning there was common ground. But he let it go, gathering up his book and his coat. She could give him what he wanted, and it wasn't just that. It was the thing he did not deserve.

He walked away from the apartment before the lease was up. Three new shirts were still in the closet. Thanksgiving would arrive soon—the day after tomorrow, in fact. He thought it would be best if he were traveling.

On to the Amtrak Station on South 15th Street. He spoke to the woman behind the counter. She suggested an itinerary. St. Louis–Chicago–Washington, D.C.–Jacksonville.

If he left in the morning, he'd arrive in Florida on Saturday, the holiday disappearing in the rattle of steel wheels on the tracks.

Fine. Thank you.

She said, "Name, please."

He could tell her Donnie Bliss. He could use his own credit cards. He didn't have to hide anymore.

Yes he did. Nothing had changed.

Moira was gone and Pup was still far away.

He reached for his new ID.

The woman behind the glass read it through bifocals.

"Bill Boardman," she said. "Hartford, Ohio."

She looked at him.

"I didn't know there was a Hartford in Ohio."

"There are two," said Bill Boardman as he counted out twenties for the fare.

ABOUT THE AUTHOR

PHOTO BY ANDREI JACKAMETS, 2007

Jim Fusilli is the author of eight novels and numerous short stories. He's also the rock and pop critic of the *Wall Street Journal*. He lives in New York City.